CHAPTER ONE

Bondawaa

"When everyone had dressed their children for the final exit from the Bundo bush, Njabu, my wife, stood out tall among the rest of the initiates. She was one of the two who had shoes on and had their hair braided," Mugbeh said proudly. "I hired the service of the best singer. When she raised the first chant, people deserted their own daughters they had dressed to come and see this unique, priceless new Bundo graduate," he added.

The hunched-backed singer's lyrics had spread the message of Njabu's beauty across Kobabu well before the new Bundo graduates and the rest of their entourage got there:

A daughter is gold
Those who long to mother an allure
Come and see Njabu
Watch her for hours
And perceive not
The full depth of her beauty
Her smiles dispel gloom
From the face of the earth
She laughs in darkness
And her teeth illuminate the entire place
When she talks
Nightingales come chanting the chorus
Live in heaven on earth forever
Lucky husband of this belle

1

Mugbeh, Bondawaa's dad, was very proud of the distinguished role he played during the Bundo initiation rites of his wife, Njabu, Bondawaa's mother. Various kinds of colourful events are held on the day that initiates make their final departure from the Bundo bush to the town. Each potential husband and his family, in collaboration with the bride-to-be's parents, will put up a grand show to mark the occasion. For poor families, the high costs associated with the initiation ceremonies make them even poorer. Sometimes it ended the education of children in primary and secondary school.

It takes a whole year or more for most prospective husbands to prepare for the initiation of their potential wives into the Bundo society. They make farms intended solely for the initiation. The crops grown on these farms: rice, okra, cassava, garden eggs, etc. are sold to businesswomen and the money is used to cover the initiation expenses. Some of the crops are also used to feed the Bundo girls throughout their stay in the bush, and to eat during the various initiation ceremonies. Some of the men, who think that the education of their children will impair the preparation for the initiation of their prospective brides, pull those children out of school.

Bondawaa's mother was the only surviving child of her mother. She was of average height, a beauty in her own right. It was when Njabu made her first visit to Ngawobu with her grandmother that Bondawaa's father fell in love with her and started to court her. A chief had already asked for her hand in marriage, but she had made no commitment to him.

2

Abbie, Njabu's younger and only sister, died at childbirth. That was her first pregnancy, and her own mother, Mbetu, delivered her. Mbetu's success as a Traditional Birth Attendant was acclaimed in Kobabu and the surrounding villages. She had been trained and certificated by the Ministry of Health and Sanitation. Also, her prowess in traditional medicine was next to none in the whole of Ngawobu chiefdom. Mbetu had medication for fibroids, infertility, fits, and almost all illnesses that affect mothers and babies. She even healed men not virile, and those bitten by snakes, and other venomous reptiles.

Abbie went into labour early in the morning of that fateful Friday. It was during the Easter vacation and Bondawaa had gone to Kobabu to help his parents with farm work. Early that Friday morning, Bondawaa, his younger brother and cousins were asked to go to the farm and ensure that marauding birds would not eat the rice that had been ploughed there.

If Abbie had delivered in time, Bondawaa's aunt would have brought the good news to them on the farm and food as well. By 4:00 pm it dawned on Bondawaa and the other bigger boys who had gone with him to the farm on that day, that all was not well in the town. Nobody had come to join them, and there was no food on the farm to eat. They had cracked and eaten cups full of palm kernel, so much that they had blisters all over their mouths.

The sun was now about to set, and the marauding birds had all gone to their resting places. "It is now safe for us to leave for the town. The birds will not come again until tomorrow morning," Bondawaa told

3

the others. They quickly washed, packed, and left. As soon as they went through the farm, they saw Abbie going ahead of them with a child strapped to her back. Bondawaa called after her and asked her to wait for them to see the baby.

"That is not Abbie, it is not possible for her to deliver the baby and bring it all the way to the bush this same day", one of Bondawaa's cousins said. They doubled their steps to catch up with the woman with the child on her back. The faster they walked the farther away the woman moved from them. To get closer, they started to run. "Ngɔ Abbie (*reference to someone slightly older than you*), you are moving unusually fast, please wait for us. We want to see the baby, and then we will go to the town together," Bondawaa and the others shouted after the strange woman.

She turned and looked at them, but her face was veiled. "Don't worry about me and the child, go to the town. I will meet you all there," she said in a nasal sound. Then she left the road and disappeared into the bush. When Bondawaa and others got to the point where the woman had walked off into the bush, they stopped and called the second time. This time the baby on her back started to cry far away in the bush. In a moment, the cry of the baby turned into the sound of an owl. Soon darkness began to fall, and a heavy breeze began to blow. While they were trying to make sense of what was going on, they heard a voice coming towards them. "Abbie has died with the baby in her womb," the crying voice announced. Bondawaa ran towards the voice with the others after him.

As they got closer, they found Njabu sprawled on the ground. "My children, I am now the only child left to my mother. My only sister has died. She could not make it through the strenuous task of childbirth. She has died with the baby in her womb," she wailed struggling to stand. After they helped her to her feet, Bondawaa told Njabu that her aunt Abbie was not dead. "She was going ahead of us just now. She went into the bush and asked us to go to the town and not worry about her and the child that was strapped to her back," he said. Njabu fell on the ground again, but this time she fainted.

When they got to the town after Njabu recovered from the shock, Bondawaa could not help noticing how quiet Kobabu was that night. Darkness had now firmly taken hold of the town but there were a few hurricane lights here and there. The town was in mourning, with sporadic crying: the voices of women, men, and children. There was a dirge coming from the Bundo bush where Abbie had died, and her body had been hidden away from the men as well as women who had not had children.

I beseech you my people
This is an enactment of the story of the great swimmer
Who swam the whole day
And drowned while approaching the end of
The expansive lake
My people see how I swam the whole day
With my daughter firmly under my armpit
Wriggling in labour

5

Twisting turning and grunting
Heavy with a poor angel who yearned
To see its first light of day
I swam fervently
Alas, as I approached the shore
Weakness crept in
We had all swum whole day
The angle stopped to kick and box any more
Clung to my arm my daughter began to gasp
I started to sink with the double load
There was wailing from the shore
The unbeatable swimmer has drowned
I continued to sink
The load pressed me down and I drowned
With child and grandchild clung to me we
drowned

The following day, mourning for Abbie and her unborn baby continued with several ceremonies. It was an abomination for a woman to die in labour, and this had not happened in Kobabu for as long as anyone could remember. They had to cleanse the town and remove Abbie's footprints. It was an elaborate event with Bundo women walking about naked to their loins, holding calabashes filled with unknown concoctions that they sprinkled across the town, on roofs, on men and women. The Sowies (*heads of the Bundo secret society*), who were dressed like warriors, carried swords, and swivelled their hips. These Sowies were flanked by a dozen and more Bundo devils. The chiming bells attached to their dark and solemn masks heightened the mournful atmosphere in Kobabu that morning.

CHAPTER TWO

Bondawaa is Circumcised

Early one morning, in December after schools had closed for Christmas, Bondawaa's maternal grandfather beckoned to him and said, "My boy let us go behind the round house and make you into a man." He was already eight years old and in standard one. The cold harmattan wind was biting deep into Bondawaa's flesh. The whole village was shrouded in freezing mist, and when someone spoke, their breath appeared like smoke from a volcano. Bondawaa followed his grandfather briskly with his knees knocking and his upper jaws beating against the lower. Behind the roundhouse stood an elderly man in a floating gown. No sooner had Bondawaa met the old man than his grandfather told him to strip himself of his clothes.

"But it is very cold this morning, why should I undress?"

"To be circumcised."

Bondawaa had secretly longed for this day, but he never thought he would be taken by surprise. His heart sank and he began to shake.

"But…but…I…I…" Bondawaa began to stammer.

"But you said he was the bravest, why is he behaving so cowardly?" the circumciser asked.

"I am not afraid; I'm merely shivering with cold. I'll get over it very soon. Just give me some time," he

8

lied. The more time Bondawaa was given the more afraid he became.

"You are allegedly the bravest of them all. If you are going to face this battle like a coward, what do you expect the ones who will come after you to do?" the circumciser rebuked.

Bondawaa walked to the low wooden stool, sat down, and spread his legs apart. He bit his lips hard and looked far away, ready for the circumciser's knife. It was a crude operation! There was no anaesthetic. What was more; they applied a stinging substance to the wound soon after the operation. In Bondawaa's own case, it was the hottest species of ginger. At that moment, he thought the application of ginger or hot pepper to the fresh wound of the circumcised was cruel. Later in life he came to learn that it was a traditional form of disinfectant.

He and the five others from the same household who had been circumcised were soon feasting on the most sumptuous of dishes. Bondawaa's grandmother was overindulgent that day. She sat by his side on the mat and fanned the dish from which they were eating. She even helped feed Bondawaa occasionally. It was a bittersweet moment. Painful, yet pleasant!

CHAPTER THREE

Bondawaa in Kobabu

Soon after Bondawaa started work as a pupil teacher, his mother was expecting a baby. She had longed for a daughter since she had Bondawaa. Bondawaa's mother had her last child, the tenth, but the sixth surviving, while he was spending long vacation in the village. The rains had been very heavy that year, and there was food shortage sweeping across the country. Some people went without rice and cassava for a whole week; others did not have a proper meal for a day or two.

Despite the famine, Bondawaa went to Kobabu and stayed there for two months. Bondawaa had a strong attachment to Kobabu because he was born there and one of the coconut trees in the village was growing right on top of his navel string. The foreskin of his male organ was buried there too.

"Bondawaa, this pregnancy has lasted unusually long; don't you think there is a big baby girl lying here in this womb?" she asked, eager to hear his opinion.

"How could I know?" he asked her.

"Well, it is because you educated people know a lot of things. Even those things that we hide from you at times," she said. She went on to tell him how experienced women and soothsayers had all assured her that she was carrying a baby girl in her womb.

"If I were you, I'd be very happy and grateful to God if He were to give me a boy again. After all, you now have a granddaughter," he teased her.

10

"Oh, what a wicked man this son of mine is. Won't you pray for me so that this one in my womb is a girl, eh? Who will wash and dress me when I die? Who will give me old clothing? A daughter is gold, Bondawaa, a daughter is gold. I don't want to be deprived of gold all my life," his mother said with tears forming clouds in her eyes.

Bondawaa told his mother after two days that she was going to deliver an ugly baby boy in three days' time. "I will be sleeping when it will happen; they will wake me up to break the news to me."

Bondawaa's dreams were nine chances to one. He had had an uninterrupted sleep until 2:30a.m, when a woman tapped on his door, talking in a loud voice. "You witch, come and see the ugly thing your mother has given birth to. He has a prick like you." That was their grandmother talking, the village's midwife. She had worked expectantly, looking forward to seeing a baby girl, despite the accuracy of Bondawaa's dreams. He grabbed a towel, wrapped it around his waist and hurried to the "Big House" where all the women of their household who were not sleeping with their husbands slept. The household's boys and girls also slept in this house. The big-headed thing was lying by the fire in the centre of the "Big House". Though Njabu had already had a granddaughter, she was still anxious to have her own bona fide daughter. One she could breastfeed for two years.

Kobabu was a beautiful village situated on sandy land. A thick forest surrounded it, and two streams flowed close by, one on the eastern side and the other to the southern side. People who believed strongly in

11

communal life lived in Kobabu. Everybody was responsible for the village children, particularly those who were going to school. Bondawaa remembered very well when every grown up in the village used to refer to him as *nya wuu mui* (*my white man*). Sometimes he was offended by the unflagging concern his townspeople showed. As a little boy, he used to see it as inquisitiveness. In those days, going to Kobabu on holidays meant facing the gauntlet of villagers. Their questions were mostly focused on his progress in school, his health, if he was well fed in Ngawobu, if the teachers were not callous and if he was going to stay long with them.

During school days when Bondawaa used to go to Kobabu for the long vacation, the boys together with the girls would sleep on a large mat, which they spread in the farmhouse. Once their millet flowered, the threat of marauding birds meant they could no longer sleep in the village at night and go to the farm early in the morning. If they did, the birds would eat up all the grains before they get there. While sleeping in the farmhouse was fun, there were things that Bondawaa disliked about it. Late at night, he would be woken up by the horrid sounds of crickets, witch birds and other nocturnal creatures. The guttural voices of the witch birds frightened him. He would hear the male tell the female:

> *I waa yo-o*
> *I waa yo-o*
> *Yombo, bimbi hu gbelƐ*
> *KƐnga tƐku wo lɔ nao-o*

Bɔngei ya fele njɔpɔ wahun siling-o

It has come-o
It has come-o
Yombo, search into the fishing net
Maybe there is a little fish there – o
In the market
Bonga is now two for one shilling – o (a herring-like fish)

Bondawaa would begin to wonder if he was the fish trapped in the net the male witch bird was informing his wife about. While some of these sounds used to instil fear in him, Bondawaa used to enjoy the voice of the *Hotoni*e (*a giant African lizard*), which calls her spouse in the early morning, to bring fire for her to warm herself. The voice of the *Hotonie* is sweet and yet melancholic. The story is that her husband deserted her several years back. In the early morning when it was very cold, the female *Hotonie* is reminded of the comfort she used to enjoy from her husband and would begin to call him to come back with fire for them to warm themselves together.

Kobabu was one of the villages notorious for witchcraft in Ngawobu chiefdom. During the dry season, the witches would poison the village's only source of drinking water and the whole village would be struck by diarrhoea and bloody stool. Children and even the adults would die in large numbers. In the rainy season the witches would cast a net round the village as a trap. Inferior witches who wanted to fly in or out would be caught in it. During any of these

13

incidences, about ten or more people would die before the master witch doctor would be asked to arrest it.

Kobabu was also well known for early harvests in Ngawobu chiefdom. The harvest season was in many ways like life in a diamond-rich town. The village would be packed full of people. Some young men and women would flock into Kobabu only for the pageantry at that time of the year. Others would come to work to get some food for their famished families back home. Petty traders would rush to Kobabu with their wares to sell for cash or to exchange them for millet. Singers and storytellers too would come to Kobabu. Despite the hunger that farmers would have experienced for the better part of the year, during harvest season they would waste food as if it would never run out again. Women would cook huge mounds of millet. It was the time of the year when mortars worked overtime pounding millet, leaving signs of abundance everywhere.

When the young people gathered in the town square at night to dance, the favourite song was *Hota nyɛnɛ neini (a stranger's liver is tasty)*. This song was a warning to strangers in Kobabu to stay in their beds at night and not wander into the witches' playground. They would begin by singing other songs first until the town square was jammed with people, and suddenly the lead-singer and drummer would pitch *Hota nyɛnɛ neini*:

> *Hota nyɛnɛ neini*
> *Kɛba mɛ bi kɔɔ pein*
> *Jee konde wi kwee*

14

Hotei yo-o
Bi nyεnie lɔ yiima
Jee konde wi kwee

A stranger's liver is tasty
You only need to have a taste
Jee konde wi kwee
The stranger yo-o
Your liver is being cooked
In the witches' cauldron
Jee konde wi kwee

The lead-singer would then go on to sing that the other parts such as the heart, the spleen, the kidney, the hind leg, etc., etc. were all in the great witches' pot cooking. The song always signalled the departure of several people from the dance. The number would begin to dwindle, leaving only the strong breed. I mean those indigenes and strangers, who knew, and were cocksure, that their liver and other parts of their body could not be cooked in a witch's cauldron. The first time Bondawaa heard this song he ran back to the house and wrapped himself in his granny's cover cloth.

"Oh, please hide me, Mbetu, they are singing a fearful song. I don't want somebody to mistake my liver for a stranger's," he told his granny still trembling.

"Is that what has driven you from the dance? Are you sure you are not a witch? If you are, better tell me now so that we can kill it before you grow up with it. Witchcraft is a terrible thing," his granny warned.

15

"But Mbetu, how can one know that he is a witch or not?"

"If you are a witch you can fly at night and can hurl terror and destruction at people."

"Oh, how I wish I were a witch, Mbetu, to fly to places, to sling terror at my enemies, those who take advantage of my age and size," Bondawaa said and soon fell asleep.

CHAPTER FOUR

Bondawaa's Grandfather

Bondawaa's granddad used to enjoy telling him about the heroic deeds of their forefathers.   His favourite heroes were Kpuivai and Ndambiwaa. As far as Bondawaa was concerned, Ndambiwaa's prowess was the stuff of myths, though many people that live in Ngawobu chiefdom confirmed that the man lived there.

His granddad only told him about the valour of these heroes when Bondawaa behaved like a weakling. Huge and gallant-looking, Bondawaa's granddad was a fearless, and industrious man – perhaps the last of the sterner breed of Ngawobu. At times, he would hold Bondawaa by the arm, raise him right up in the air, shake, and then swing him right round his head, put him down laughing and then say, "_Siyɔɔ_ (_an expression of disappointment_), this would not have survived if he was born in the inter-tribal warring days. If he did, he would have died somebody's domestic slave." He would laugh for a long time, shake his head, and ask Bondawaa, "You mean the first son of a warrior's grandson, and you are so weak?"

Now, Ngawobu is known across Simbeck and beyond for producing fine academics, brilliant politicians, outstanding women of international repute, and renowned artists. One time in an august gathering in the Ngawobu Court Barrie, the Chairman, a son of the soil, said rather immodestly, that one only needed

17

a week's stay in Ngawobu chiefdom, and he or she would be alright.

One day, during Bondawaa's early days in secondary school, he accompanied the school's football team to play a friendly match against a neighbouring school. They were beaten twice. They beat them on the pitch and off. Most of them sustained wounds. When they returned Bondawaa's granddad was upset by the news.

"How many of you went with the team?"

"Oh, not many, only thirty supporters and eighteen members of the football team," Bondawaa said defensively. His granddad began to laugh.

"Did you say forty-eight? That number was enough to beat the whole of the host school and everybody in the town", he said now looking serious.

"Granddad, how can you say that?" Bondawaa asked feeling offended.

"Come on boy, no need to fly into a temper. I will tell you what Ndambiwaa did to a mammoth crowd from five villages combined, and then you will understand what I mean."

"There you are and your Ndambiwaa again!"

"Look, child, you must listen to this incident, and then you will understand that you should not have allowed yourselves to be beaten like a bunch of women. See how shameful it is that you have all come back with wounds and blisters, wagging your tails between your legs like cowardly dogs."

"Granddad, please-ee!"

"You see, Ndambiwaa used to go miles and miles away to other villages and take their cattle from them

18

by force. A whole village of about thirty, forty men would attack him, but he would beat them all up and bring their cattle home with him".

"But granddad, he was wrong in doing that. That was the law of the jungle; he was misusing the strength that God gave him."

"Please let us not talk about right and wrong now, for your own generation knows more wrongs than rights".

"What do you mean?"

"Wait and see, one fine day the whole world will be at war with each other with nobody to talk peace. Even the big empires will be fully engaged."

"The world is now too civilized to allow that kind of situation to arise," Bondawaa said, giggling with boyish mirth.

"You know what? When we returned from the First World War, considering the human and material destruction the so-called civilized world exposed the whole world to, we thought a similar war would not be provoked in a hurry, but the Second World War was not too long in coming. So, what are you talking about?"

"I think the Second World War taught everyone who was involved in it and their backers a much bitter lesson, a lesson that will caution them again and again," Bondawaa said. "Ndambiwaa was a menace to those villages. You mean they allowed him to continue to be a bother to them like that?" he asked his granddad angrily.

"The people came together one day and worked out a strategy to catch their enemy once and for all. They

19

devised a way of communicating with everyone in the affected villages whenever Ndambiwaa was around. "He can beat a village or two but not several villages put together," they all agreed.

"They decided to use smoke as a channel to inform one another of the presence of Ndambiwaa in their midst. Before the meeting broke off, every village had been asked to stack huge piles of wood at strategic places and be ready to set them ablaze when they saw this monster. The smoke would give an idea of the village Ndambiwaa wanted to rob. For four months young men kept guard at observation posts, poised and ready for the enemy, their tormentor, Ndambiwaa!"

But Bondawaa was still trying to figure out the relationship between their being beaten at a football match and the barbaric behaviour of this monstrous hero.

"Two weeks into the fifth month after his last exploit, and it was now early dry season when the villagers are less busy and have ample time for pastime, Ndambiwaa was ready to return to his usual hunt. He got there at early dawn. He crossed several observation posts under the cloak of darkness. He had planned to strike in the largest village where he was sure he would herd away about forty to sixty goats and sheep together." Bondawaa's granddad paused and looked at his grandson to see how much effect the story was having on him.

"I pray that they catch and kill this ogre this time," Bondawaa shouted.

"But he is your kinsman, the giant and pride of Ngawobu."

"It is a pity that he hails from Ngawobu. I hate him. I am not proud of him at all."

Bondawaa's granddad laughed at his grandson quietly and resumed the story, "Before he entered his target village huge clouds of smoke were already shrouding the sky behind him. The tall, gigantic creature was least aware of this development. When he arrived at the village, he asked the few young men who were there to help him herd the cattle together, after he had asked the women to cook for him to eat." Bondawaa was feeling uncomfortable and wanted his granddad to stop, but at the same time he wanted to know the end of this audacious monster.

"While they were herding the cattle together and the women were cooking for Ndambiwaa, the village was surrounded by hundreds of able-bodied young men. After eating and resting, he set out for Ngawobu. Right in the outskirts of the village he was confronted by a group of men.

"Where did you get all these cattle from?" their spokesman asked.

"From the village right behind me; would you like to help me drive them across the first four villages?" he asked the spokesman and laughed cynically.

"No, I am not going to be a party to your banditry," the spokesman answered, and laughed in a provocative way.

"Watch your words young man; else I will force you to help me drive these animals right to my destination."

"A black lie, in fact on my honour as a member of the *Poro* (a *male secret society common in some west*

21

African countries) society, you will not take these animals beyond this point," the young man said and stood right in the way of Ndambiwaa. The other men began to drive the cattle back to the village. Ndambiwaa became extremely angry and began to bray like a horse. A band of men rushed at him, and soon the number of attackers began to swell from ten to thirty, fifty, one hundred, two hundred, three hundred - as men continued to emerge from the bush. He fought them for about two hours before they finally conquered him." Bondawaa became so excited, that he started to jump up and down; as he did this, his granddad was laughing at him quietly.

"No plant has ever grown in the place where that battle took place," Granddad Jaiah said and began to squeeze Bondawaa's right hand, laughing. He laughed frenziedly, and for a long time. Bondawaa became impatient.

"What did they do to him after they had captured him?"

"Oh, they tied his limbs together, put him in the sun and discussed what to do with him."

"They should have burnt him alive."

"Nothing of that, they decided to cook and eat him."

"But that is cannibalism!"

"Yes, but of a ritualistic nature, it was a way of infusing his strength into the men of those villages and their next generation."

"I cannot see how his strength could have been transferred in that way."

"You cannot understand my child. You need to be schooled on this for you to understand it." Granddad said the people took the tied-up Ndambiwaa to their secret bush, left a strong, sturdy-built man with a club in charge of him, while they all went back to their different villages to bring utensils, herbs, and other paraphernalia they needed for the ritual. As they all departed, Ndambiwaa turned his head away from his guard and smiled happily. The birds were singing in the heart of this mysterious forest, and soon the wind began to blow gently. There was now the voice of a praise singer filling the air, accompanied by a talking drum. The drum and the praise singer in unison recounted the names and prowess of their heroes. As the descant and the voices of the people drew near, the guard jumped from his seat and began to dance and sway the club to the rhythm of the drum.

Ndambiwaa looked at the guard carefully while he was busy dancing. "What a magnificent dancer, he said to himself. But I need waste no more time." He tore the ropes off his limbs and leaped from the ground; by the time the guard could realize what was happening, Ndambiwaa grabbed the club from him, seized him by the hand and squeezed his throat until he became lifeless. To make sure the guard was not faking death; Ndambiwaa clubbed his head to a pulp and left his lifeless body oozing blood through the nostrils and ears, as he disappeared into the forest.

"Oh blood, blood, blood", Bondawaa said and shut his eyes. His granddad began to laugh at him. He had never seen him laugh like this. The old man got up and entered his room slowly. When he returned, he was still laughing quietly. "You should not regard that single killing and the oozing of the blood of one person

23

as anything dreadful. I wish you had lived at the time Ngombu Koma invaded Belloh", granddad switched to the exploit of another of his favourite heroes. He had stopped laughing and his face was now very serious. "Your face now wears an awesome kind of seriousness. I guess you are not going to freeze my blood with a more unpleasant story".

"I am not doing this to horrify you, my child. You must learn about the heroes of your land, and their prowess. Your mind should feed on the pleasant and the unpleasant accounts of your people. That will give you a strong and well-balanced personality," his granddad said as he grabbed his hand and began to squeeze it assuredly. The town was getting quieter, with most of the people already gone to bed. The moon was shining so brightly that one could see the palm of his hand.

According to granddad, Ngombu Koma, a fearless warrior from Mojoijoi, embarked on an ambitious siege of Ngawobu chiefdom. He had attacked and plundered four villages in the chiefdom and was now camped at the fifth, from where he sent a message to Ngawobu town to get ready for him.

While such a heinous threat was hanging over the people of Ngawobu, Kpuivai, their foremost warrior, was away with his team of warriors, fighting as mercenaries for another chiefdom. The news of Ngombu Koma's intention struck Ngawobu like thunder. Ngombu Koma's fame as a warrior was known far and wide. A lot of mysterious things were said about him. How he could disappear from his enemies, how he could change into an elephant, a lion,

24

or even a boa constrictor in the battlefield and how he was invulnerable to sword and bullet.

"If he gets here and there is nobody like Kpuivai to challenge him, that will be the end of us all" the Elders said at a meeting. They sent an emissary to call Kpuivai and his team back home. While they were waiting for them to come back, Ngawobu was tense and in deep fear. The walls around the town were shut to strangers and the women went about only in the company of junior warriors. The atmosphere was very tense and uncertain, indeed. If a child cried, its mother would quickly throw her breast into its mouth. Even the chickens became aware of the danger that loomed over Ngawobu. They never cackled as before but buried themselves deep in the dust exposing only their heads. The days became unusually long, and the people of Ngawobu lived in abysmal fear.

The sound of horn blowing began to cut through the air and register in the hearts of the people. The whole town was thrown into confusion. Women ran into their houses, some clustered in the doorways, scrambling to get inside. Babies got choked on their mothers' backs. Dogs went barking in all directions, chickens flew about cackling irritatingly. A warrior was coming to Ngawobu, being announced by his horn blower. Nobody knew yet who he was. "Is this the great Ngombu Koma coming to destroy Ngawobu before Kpuivai is here with his team? Our gods, what laws have we violated to deserve a humiliation such as this? Is the only son of the great swimmer going to drown just a few feet away from the bank? What will he tell the world when he gets the news?" a retired warrior was saying.

The horn blast was now very near, echoing in every big tree in the forest surrounding Ngawobu. Hearts were throbbing as people quivered and sweated profusely in hiding. The horn blowing could be heard very clearly now:

> *Kpuivai*
> *Kpuivai*
> *Kpuivai*
> *Tɛ Ngɔmbu Koma waa*
> *Kɔlei wuma Ngawo leingaa ma*

> *Kpuivai*
> *Kpuivai*
> *Kpuivai they say*
> *Ngombu Koma has come to make*
> *The children of Ngawo catch fever*

Kpuivai's horn blower was announcing him as he approached his homeland to save her from the impending ravage of an over-ambitious warrior. The message of the horn blowing was now distinct. Perhaps, it had all along been clear, but everybody was too scared to listen to it very carefully. The message of this very horn blowing had in time past, always been recognized by the sons and daughters of Ngawobu from miles and miles away, and they would climb tall trees along the roads to give ovation to their greatest warrior, Kpuivai returning victorious from wars. Women would stream from houses, some with their

26

babies' mouths glued to their breasts, to wave and smile to Kpuivai as he entered Ngawobu. The children too would take their positions in less strategic places to smile to their idol. Now, as this same horn blowing announced Kpuivai even on to the outskirts of Ngawobu, nobody seemed to recognize and understand the message, save this retired warrior.

"Come out of hiding everybody! Stop suffocating our babies to death. The invincible son of Ngawobu is here." Gbandabla, the retired warrior, announced. The town was soon bustling with life once more, even with Ngombu Koma seven miles away, poised to attack them.

At this point, Granddad began to smile broadly. "You are too full of fear, you weakling. I can see your eyes are hollow with fear," Granddad teased Bondawaa.

"You are right, but what happened when Kpuivai came?" Granddad told Bondawaa that Ngombu Koma was such a brave and daring warrior that when Kpuivai and his team of warriors met him at Belloh on the first day, they fought for a whole day with no side gaining supremacy. Bondawaa's stomach rumbled at this point of the tale. He asked his granddad to accompany him to the latrine – a small pit latrine some twenty yards away from the house. As Bondawaa squatted there alone, with his granddad waiting a reasonable distance away, he began to wonder how a warrior, perhaps from a second-rate chiefdom, could come and subdue a chiefdom such as Ngawobu. He was now praying fervently that the tale should not end in favour of

Ngombu Koma that he forgot about his mission to the toilet entirely.

"Are you excreting stone?" His granddad asked impatiently.

"No *Maada* (*granddad*), I am praying for Kpuivai, he will beat Ngombu Koma on the second day. You wait and see," he said sombrely.

"You don't need to cry yet; you don't know if your great granduncle is going to beat or not. Wait and see". They went back to the veranda. The hurricane lamp had become dim. Bondawaa rushed into the room, came back with a pint of kerosene, and refilled it.

"Kpuivai changed his strategy the next day. Belloh was by the River Tɛbɛlɛh. He set a contingent of his war boys behind the river to wait for whoever wanted to escape across it. Early in the morning he mounted the fortifications and was waiting there patiently for Ngombu Koma." he told his grandson. "Very sure of himself that morning, he always had been, Ngombu Koma embarked on a tour round the fortifications. As he went round his horn blower announced him:

> *Ngɔmbu Koma*
> *Ngɔmbu Koma*
> *Gbanawulii*
> *Kai nya mui*
> *Fulii hijia ye*
>
> *Ngombu Koma*
> *Ngombu Koma*
> *The spitting cobra*
> *The venomous snake*

The sun has risen.

Soon, Ngombu Koma was coming close to Kpuivai with his horn blower still pumping air of superiority into him:

Ngɔmbu Koma
Ngɔmbu Koma
Gbandia
Masubawai

Ngombu Koma
Ngombu Koma
The hot-headed
The super dangerous

As Ngombu Koma approached where Kpuivai had laid an ambush fuming and ululating, Kpuivai landed right in front of him, and a duel ensued. For twenty minutes both men fought equally. The morning sun was now getting hot, and both warriors were already bathing in their own sweat. The early birds had now had their breakfast and were singing happily, drying their feathers in the sun. The Tɛbɛlɛh River was spluttering in the background. As the monkeys began to cackle, the hero emerged; Kpuivai's sword landed on Ngombu Koma's right shoulder. He dropped his sword and went down on his knees; he had received a lethal blow.

Horn blowers, like some people, were quick to change their loyalty. They never followed a falling star, and so he quickly changed his message:

Kɔleiwua Ngombu Koma ma
Kɔleiwua Ngɔmbu Koma ma

Ngombu Koma has caught fever
Ngombu Koma has caught fever

As was typical of warriors in those days, Kpuivai announced himself and set Belloh, the coveted village, ablaze.

Nyamia–o Kpuivai
Nyamia–o Kpuivai
Ngi Belloh gbia ha
Ngɔmbu Koma yeya
Faa numuina gbi ngi wooma mɔ a biye
Tao bi longɔ a bi lɛvui
Gbia tei jihun bi lii

It is me-o, Kpuivai
It is me-o, Kpuivai
From today I have redeemed
Belloh from Ngombu Koma
I therefore warn all those
Who have been fighting on his side
And love their lives
To flee this village
And now

Most of Ngombu Koma's warriors and war boys plunged into the river; the ones who managed to swim across had their heads cut off as soon as they stepped

30

out of the river. It was a real carnage! "For a whole week the River Tɛbɛlɛh was blood red from Belloh to Ngawobu and beyond," his granddad concluded the tale, tittering. Bondawaa became terrified, and an unusual chill began to consume him.

Bondawaa's granddad had two humourous stories that he was very fond of. When he had told Bondawaa a couple of horror stories, he would bring in a light relief for him.

One of the funny stories was about Rat and Cat.

Rat was looking for food for his family one day when he unexpectedly ran into cat. It was the lean period, and that rainy season, the animal kingdom was going through severe famine. It had rained non-stop for four days, and all these days the families of both cat and rat had not had any solid food to eat. Out of desperation, both animals had gone out in the heavy and breezy rain to fend for their families. As he moved about looking for food, his eyes dim and legs wobbling, rat saw cat coming from a distance not too far from him. He decided not to run because he did not have much energy left in him. He worked on a quick disguise. He increased the size of his ears, stretched them in such a way that they made him look unusually big and fearful. His manes all stood up on his back, and his beard was like thorns. Satisfied with what he had done, rat stood there looking away.

Cat came closer but was not sure of the animal in front of him.

31

"A squirrel, a badger, a cutting grass?" cat began to ask himself. For sure he had never seen a rat as big and fearful.

"What is your name?" cat asked the rat.

"*Yone*" (*the great one*), rat said.

"*Yone*, where are you from and where are you going to?"

"From the forest, and I am going to the desert in search of a camel for my family to eat."

"What an absurdity! How can an animal as small as this fetch a camel for his family? Of course, this cannot be a rat," the cat said to himself. As they went along conversing, cat became frightened the more, "A small animal that feeds on camels, where does his power lie?" he asked himself.

"*Yone*, my family and I have not eaten for four days now, I want to go with you to the dessert, and maybe we could find a baby camel for me to bring home for my family." Rat never fell for the phony helplessness that cat was displaying; in fact, he did not want cat to come very close, because he knew every rodent by its body odour.

"I have no problem with that, just wait here for me to bring two ropes that we will use to bring the mother and baby camels home," rat said.

"How far away is the rope?"

"Oh, not too far, I think it is only fifty steps away from here." Suddenly, rat started counting his steps towards a burrow he had seen in view. Before cat could understand what was happening, rat ran into the hole. Cat ran towards the hole and stood at the entrance irritated, calling "*Yone – Yone, Yone, Yone?*"

******

One day, Bondawaa's granddad told him about yesterday, comparing it with today.

"Bondawaa," he called him, "A lot of things have changed today. I am happy that I'm approaching my grave," he said wearily. "But at the same time, I am sad that I am leaving people like you behind, for I am pretty sure these changes are going to hit you harder," he concluded, bearing a serious countenance. Bondawaa had always feared his granddad when he had a countenance such as that. He became perplexed.

"Won't you send me manna from your grave when you are dead, Granddad, please?" Bondawaa knew how to drive this fearsome countenance from his granddad.

"Manna from my grave?" he smiled. "When a community goes bad, its neighbours are bound to be affected," he said, laughing weakly. "Let us take the story of the orphan who was constantly maltreated by her stepmother. She would over-work her, beat and underfeed her. When this persisted, the poor girl became a mere skeleton. One day her late mother appeared to her while she was crying and carrying a large pile of clothes to the river to wash, feeling extremely hungry." His granddad paused and breathed heavily. Bondawaa became frightened and funny images began to cross his mind's eye. A brief silence invaded them, and Granddad was sort of metamorphosing into a ghost.

"Granddad!" Bondawaa yelled.

33

"She promised her daughter riches, and the next day this poor orphan girl became the richest person in the whole chiefdom, he resumed."

"She was?" Bondawaa asked, excited. "Of course, she was."

"Ah, it was remarkable, wasn't it?"

"Indeed, it was, but a lot of changes have taken place in the next world too. Those people have been disarmed just like us," his granddad said again with a serious countenance. "Take the case of all those orphans who are now being enslaved by their extended family members. Can any of their parents emerge from the grave and give them even a crumb of bread? What about those who are being killed innocently these days, some for power? Won't they strike their enemies on the heads with truncheons? My boy, I think a considerable change is going on in the world of the dead as well," the old man said and was now laughing. But it was a laugh of gloom. Bondawaa became worried.

"If you look around today you can see that some people are extremely wealthy and others very poor. Why?" his granddad asked.

"Because some work hard while others are lazy," he answered.

"Work hard, eh? But how many people are working even much harder and yet they are not rich?"

"Granddad you are right! You are very strong and have been working very hard right through your life, but you are not rich," Bondawaa said, rather naïvely.

"Yes, it is because I care for my people. I feed every one of them. I give a decent burial to any one of

34

them who dies. I feed the ancestors lavishly. And not only that, but every stranger also that comes to Ngawobu must eat food prepared from my pot. Before my neighbour hungers and goes about in tattered clothes, let me first hunger and look haggard and wretched. We should be our brothers' keepers," his granddad said and looked at him straight in the face and began to laugh. As usual, he laughed until tears began to run down his eyes.

Bondawaa felt embarrassed to the extent that his eyes started to shed tears too.

"Look, Bondawaa, it is not yet time for you to start crying about these changes. You don't even know yet what their implications are. I laugh about them in tears because of the mixed feelings I have about them. If I should die now, I will be freed from the entire burden, but will leave my loved ones behind to battle with these changes," his granddad said, now wiping the tears from his eyes and snort from his nostrils.

"Are you worried about your children or about me"?

"I am worried about you, your children, and their own children. My children too are on the way out. The brunt of these changes will be felt from your own time onwards." It was now late in the evening; the other members of the family had gone to bed. The moon was shining brightly; it was a dry season night. The owls were hooting, the vampire bats making their clicking sounds, casting ominous sensation on the luminous, serene atmosphere. Bondawaa became so frightened by all these nocturnal noises that his heart began to pound; he pressed his granddad's hand hard.

35

"I know you are frightened by those sounds of the witches and wizards, but we have yet a lot to talk about. I can see that you are fast growing into manhood, and everyone says you are doing very well in school; whatever that means I don't know." Bondawaa smiled, feeling both elated and embarrassed. He was only fourteen years old and in form two. "As you are growing into manhood, and learning fast the ingenuity of the white man, I feel obliged to warn you." His granddad was looking at the ceiling and fidgeting with his beard.

Suddenly, he rose from his seat and began to pace the veranda thoughtfully, walking away from Bondawaa. When he turned round to face Bondawaa, he said "Being the first child of your father, and the first grandchild of the Ndoma family, you should be the corner stone upon which the family should be built after me and your father. You must, therefore, be your brothers' keeper. Your family should not only be your wife and children, but whoever looks up to you for help. Care for thy brethren. Let the new ways you are learning in school not suck out of you the spirit of communalism." His granddad was now standing right over him. He grabbed Bondawaa's hand and began to squeeze it gently.

"This new virus, individualism, must not be allowed to breed in your heart. It is destroying our communities. It is not enough for you to earn the wealth of the whole world. Your happiness should be heightened by the happiness of others. But if you are the only happy man in a community of a thousand people, your happiness will limp on one leg," the old man said. Bondawaa yawned, his tender mind struggling to absorb the octogenarian lesson he has had from his granddad. They both quietly left the veranda and headed for their different bedrooms.

In addition to the lessons, he occasionally had from his granddad, the culture of communal life was heavily imparted to children while Bondawaa was growing up in Kobabu. It was taught by parents, the community, and the secret societies. When his maternal granddad died, Bondawaa debated the relevance of communal life regarding funeral rites with his mother. He observed that some family members and friends had come to the funeral with mere twenty Dabras, and others with nothing. Yet, they decided to stay with the bereaved family until the seventh day ceremonies were conducted before departing to their various villages. And all those days they would eat three times a day and some were even served drinks such as palm and bamboo wine.

Bondawaa did not quite understand the rationale behind a practice such as that. He therefore called his mother aside on the third day of the bereavement to register his dissatisfaction.

"I cannot understand why mourners come with pittance, some with nothing and yet you allow them to stay for as long as four, five, six days. I think that is unfair to us. Any external mourner who pays a mourner's kola of less than one hundred Dabras should be encouraged to go home and come back on the day prior to the seventh day ceremonies," Bondawaa said, quite angry.

"Please do not let anyone hear such words from your mouth. Such an act is an abomination. But I know that this outlandish idea is due to your long affiliation with foreign cultures. I wonder how you will behave when you go to college in the Whiteman's country and come back," Njabu said.

"I am only trying to advise you people how to sort out things in the best way possible. I can see you running out of resources before the seventh day ceremonies, and that will be, well, very bad, don't you think so, Njabu?" Bondawaa asked hesitantly.

"You can see that this house and the others surrounding it are full of mourners. But no one has gone hungry since your granddad died. Yes, some come with no money at all, but they come with rice, some with chickens, and some with pepper, palm oil, onions, and whatever they can afford. Some will even be coming with goats and sheep; it is just a matter of time. There are those who fetch water and firewood. Some cook and warm water for the other mourners to bathe. At night, some keep mini vigil, warming up for the final vigil, which takes place on the sixth night. Money is not what we look for in a situation such as this," Njabu said.

The vigil was a great success, the kind that Bondawaa had never seen for a long time. Masked devils were brought from three neighbouring villages, and each had an entourage of more than thirty people. Each group brought their own uncooked food items: rice, palm oil, pepper, salt, onions, vegetables, chickens, and a big he-goat. On top of that, each group also paid a funeral cola of at least one thousand

Dabras. Above all, Bondawaa was enthused by what happened on the sixth and the seventh days following his grandfather's death.

CHAPTER FIVE

Saffa the Hero

Among all of them who grew up together at Ngawobu, Saffa had always considered himself their superior, the hero. He had always thought that his manhood was invincible and had tried to prove this everywhere: on the football field, in the dance hall, at play, in debates, in the classroom, everywhere. He was to a large extent, an all-rounder.

Saffa was the finest player in a friendly football match between Ngawobu High School and Bongama Secondary School. He led his team and school to victory. Both sides had played without a goal until five minutes to the final whistle when Saffa collected the ball, dribbled it through the opponent's defence and launched it into their net. The sun was now hanging over the horizon, with its red rays shimmering on the green vegetation beneath it, the birds were singing goodbye to the day in melodious voices, while the gentle wind of the early rainy season evening swept across the massive field. All the spectators rushed into the field, everyone trying hard to shake Saffa's hand.

When the whistle was blown to mark the end of the match, Saffa was carried to the town shoulder high, with the girls singing his praises, fanning him, and wiping sweat from his body with their headdresses. Among his numerous virtues, he had also always played the lead role in plays staged by the school's drama group. That was Saffa, the hero of his peers, the superior, the brave, and the foolhardy.

However, like most heroes, Saffa was guilty of arrogance, a trait that created a rift between him and some of his friends. In form four when he was vying for the position of school prefect with seven other pupils, he made a tragic mistake when he said, "I must be an extra-ordinary pupil to be nominated for the position of prefect by all the staff after being only two terms in the school; how about those who have been here three years before me?" His best friends canvassed against him. He wanted this position very badly as a boost to his budding popularity so when he lost it, he wept openly. Some of his darlings wept with him.

Saffa was playing the most recent Congolese music on his record player. The time was 7:00 pm and the rest of the boarding pupils, apart from fifth formers, had gone to the old school compound to study when a little boy ran into their dormitory, glowing with happiness, to announce the arrival of his baby boy.

"What good news!" Saffa said and rushed to the town to see his new arrival. All his colleagues rushed after him. The child was a hefty creature with a large mouth, fat nose and bulging eyes. "If your father drinks a carton of beer per day, you drink two; if he plays football for his school, you play it for your country; like father like son," they joked with the child and went back to their dormitory.

All fifth formers were asked out of that dormitory the next day. Returning to the dorm after seeing his child, Saffa bought all types of drinks to celebrate the birth of his first child with Hannah. The child they all regarded as his first legal child with a woman. They drank drunk. When every drunk had slept, even Saffa, Keifa began to praise-sing, with Bondawaa ululating. He had always thought of being a warrior, answering to praise songs and dancing to horn blowing.

Keifa went on to sing:

Jojo – ooo
Bondawaa –yo- ooo
O Bondawaa yo – o –oo
You the little bird by the wayside
The man who eats birds with their feathers on
The darkest river
The whirlpool of Moigele River
The women's favourite man
The children's father
The enemies are closing in on you

Bondawaa yelled to each line of the praise song, as if the singer was miles and miles away from him. The noise upset the warden of boys. He left his residence quietly to come and catch the rabble-rousers red-handed. The dorm was one of the surviving buildings of the Bible College that was in Ngawobu a century ago. It had a funny architecture in the opinion of many townspeople, concrete from the base right up to one's shoulder and wood from there to the lintel, with roof made of bamboo thatch. Steps leading into the dorm were a pile of rocks. As soon as the warden flashed his torchlight to see how he could balance his steps among the rocks, Bondawaa sensed him and asked Keifa to pretend to be sleeping. "Keifa sleep!" he warned. He 'slept' without asking why. As for Bondawaa, he was already snoring. This cunning and rustic behaviour, particularly on a Christian mission campus, infuriated the dean so much so that he lost control of himself and started using unprintable words against the boys. But it was all in vain, none of them reacted.

The repercussion of this primitive act was eviction. The following morning the principal came to the male dormitory and put up a notice informing all male fifth formers to vacate at the end of that day. A week or two before this incident, most of them had already packed their personal belongings and taken them home. Those who were not natives of Ngawobu took theirs to their friends. They were only waiting for the graduation ceremonies, in particular the graduation dance.

Graduation dance was what every fifth former looked forward to passionately in those days. The Graduation dance more than anything else, and the "graduate-piece!" It was an occasion of extravagance even on the part of poor parents. Parents threw extravagant parties; others wore ashobi (*uniform dress worn on festive occasions*) and hired bands of singers and dancers to entertain them during the ceremonies. What was more, the "graduate-piece" served as a barometer to test the fidelity of boyfriends to girlfriends and vice versa.

The cream of every graduation dance was the "graduate-piece." This was a piece of music played specifically for the graduates and their partners to dance to. The music for the graduate-piece was normally chosen by the graduates and was usually played after mid-night. During their own time,

43

Bondawaa had to choose between dancing the graduate-piece with a Sugar Mammy girlfriend, (*a girlfriend much older than the male friend*) Matu, and a nineteen-year-old, Gbessay. His dilemma was enormous!

Bondawaa first met Matu on a Friday evening. He was returning home from the school compound after a hard day's holiday job. It was the rainy season, but that Friday was sunny. A gentle wind was blowing across the grassland where they met, and the leaves were dancing uncontrollably in the golden beam of the fading sun. The cacophonous voices of the birds, crickets and other creatures were bidding farewell to the reddish sun that was now sitting on the edge of the horizon in the far west. All of this synchronized with the rattling of the wind. Matu mesmerized Bondawaa with alluring smiles, and suddenly a monkey began to chatter close by, rendering him transfixed, as he squinted his eyes to take in this fascinating atmosphere.

"Do you live in Ngawobu?" Matu asked Bondawaa.

"I have lived here most of my life," he answered, timidly.

"But I have never seen you here before."

"You are a newcomer that is why. I know almost everybody in this town."

"I am Matu; I was born here but have been in the diamond mine for a good number of years."

"I am Bondawaa, a pupil at Ngawobu High."

"Which family do you belong to?"

"The Ndoma family."

44

"Your uncle has been chasing me since I arrived in this town. Meet me at home tonight, I will tell you the details. I live in the house directly facing the Court Barray from the left. Will you come?"

"Sure," Bondawaa said, but she never saw him again until after a week. The next time they met, it was in the marketplace. He had gone there to buy some rice and vegetables. She rushed at Bondawaa as soon as she saw him, held him by the hand and began to smile in his face.

"Handsome youth are normally sly, eh? Why didn't you come to my house the other day as promised?"

"I did not know what to tell your husband if I had met him there," he said in a coarse voice.

"I would not have invited you to my house if my husband was there, your stupid fool," she squeezed his hand and giggled. Several eyes were now on them. Bondawaa became nervous, while Matu felt elated. She embraced and kissed him on the cheek. His heart began to beat fast.

"You must come tonight, if not I will come and take you willy-nilly. I know your house," she said and patted Bondawaa on his back gently. He left the marketplace a confused man.

The night following their meeting in the market, Matu and Bondawaa were in her bed together. He did not take his clothes off. He was very tense and cursing himself for foolishly walking into her carnal trap. He had had all kinds of discussions with his peers about sex before, but never had a practical experience. Matu became fidgety, kissing, caressing and massaging Bondawaa. He responded to each gesture half-

45

heartedly and tried weakly to get away from her grip. At one point he broke loose and ran towards the firmly locked door. Matu ran after him and stood in front of him nude. As he surveyed her nudity, he realized suddenly that he was in another world, a world of real, reckless infatuation. His mind quickly ran to the Biblical story of the Garden of Aden, and perceived Matu as the Serpent telling him to partake of the "fruit of knowledge". Should he surrender his virginity to this desperate beauty ready to devour him; is there any way he could now escape from this trap?

He walked back to the bed in a brand-new mind; ready for another *rite de passage*, loss of virginity to crown his status as *Sowohini* (*a graduate from the Poro society*), which according to his ethnic group, allows him to have an affair with a woman who has joined the female version of that secret society, Bundo. He lay flat on his face and was trying to erase from his mind what he had just seen at the door. Matu sat by his side and began to weep quietly.

"Don't you love me, Bondawaa?" she asked.

"I do, Matu," he said, with an abrasive voice.

"Then please show your love to me", she said, still weeping. After he showed his love to her, they both lay in bed looking in different directions. Suddenly, Bondawaa became very frightened and overwhelmed by a strong sense of remorse. "Where will this strange experience lead me?" he asked himself. Matu was very beautiful, a superb creation of God. She was fair complexioned, tall, slender with a dimple on each cheek and on the chin. Her lips were reedy, and her mouth was home of perfect dentition. This made her

46

the attraction of every male that was reasonably employed in Ngawobu, and poor Bondawaa their envy.

Gbessay was Matu's rival for Bondawaa's "graduate-piece." Exactly six months to the graduation ceremonies Matu moved to Kwabu, a provincial headquarters where, she said, there was a greater market for her businesses. Just one week to the graduation dance she came to Ngawobu and informed Bondawaa that she was sorry she would not be present for the dance, and that he should forgive her for whatever inconvenience her late notice would cause him. He was now free to ask Gbessay to stay for the dance.

To gain popularity some graduates invited two or more girlfriends only to dance the "graduate-peace" with one. In those days, every schoolgirl looked forward to dancing a "graduate-piece" with a young school-leaver, no matter how inconsequential the school-lever was. The girls hardly turned down a request to dance a "graduate-piece", even if they knew a series of girls were lined up for the piece with the same school-leaver. They would always try their luck.

Gbessay brought her belongings to Bondawaa's house early on the day of the graduation dance. He and some colleagues had spent three hours playing the game of scrabble together. He later joined Gbessay, and they were now together in the parlour when a friend came pent-up and called him aside and said, "Look, this Matu woman is a terrible joker. She is already here for your graduation dance with two of her friends." Bondawaa's heart leapt into his mouth. He

47

went back to Gbessay in the parlour pale, his pressure already very high.

"Why are you looking sick quite suddenly, my sweetheart?" Gbessay asked. Bondawaa rose, headed for his bedroom and went straight to bed. Not long, he began to have a nightmare. He saw a man drunk and being tossed about by a band of women. The drunk kicked in the air and fell, the women milled around him and stripped him down to his briefs and began to tweak him all over the body. As they were doing that to him, he started to yell. A crowd gathered around them, and he began to struggle to his feet. Each time he got up he crashed to the ground. Bondawaa began to yell at the crowd to leave the drunk alone.

"Bondawaa, Bondawaa what is the matter with you?" Gbessay began to shake him frantically.

"If I say let's stay here at home and enjoy our own graduation dance quietly, will you accept?" he asked, smiling at Gbessay grimly.

"Why should we do that, my dear?"

"It is because I was in the middle of a dream about the dance when you woke me, a sort of trance; it was not pleasant at all."

"Bondawaa, what is troubling you? Tell me, why should I miss dancing the "graduate-piece" with you? I am sure you did not ask me to stay for the graduation dance for you to humiliate me like this." Gbessay began to weep softly. Bondawaa came down from the bed gingerly and took Gbessay in his arms.

"Come on cry-baby, you know I can always stick out my neck to protect and make you happy," he said breathlessly. "What is at stake this time? You are

48

hiding something from me. Please be brave as usual and tell me what is going on."

Before the dance started, Bondawaa had decided to drink heavily, to the extent that he could not even walk. He wanted to be over-drunk before the long awaited "graduate-piece" so that he would be lying in some corner throwing up while it would all happen. But aside from the huge quantity of beer that he gulped; he was still sober.

That year's graduation dance was incomparable. Daughters and sons of very wealthy and influential parents were among those graduating. It was rumoured that that year was going to experience a graduation of fashionable young people. Whatever that meant, was what attracted the generality of young people to Ngawobu: pupils from other secondary schools far and near, students from university colleges, teacher training colleges, and vocational institutions. Parents young and old, literate, and illiterate: they all converged on Ngawobu. The hearsay was that even the dead rose from their graves to come and attend this much talked about, this much publicized graduation dance.

Keifa had graduated from secondary school a year before Bondawaa. During his graduation ceremony, his uncle Bengeh, who was a very successful businessman, brought to Ngawobu for the first time a dance band to play live at his nephew's graduation dance. The Super Dupper Combo Kings, one of the leading pop bands in Simbeck at the time, never played outside the capital city and the three provincial headquarters, but here they were, playing with all their might and skills in Ngawobu, a chiefdom headquarters. The gossip that continued to linger on after the entire occasion was that money can do anything under the sun.

The time was 1:30 am and it was time for the "graduate-piece". The Master of Ceremonies (MC) was Saffa. The hall was too small to take all who attended the dance that night, even though huts were constructed on three sides of it to provide more space, especially for the VIPs. The night had an aura of conviviality; there were spates of traditional dancing here and there by people who considered ball dance as foreign and somewhat boring.

The stench of alcohol and nicotine hung heavily in the air. "The disk is Jesus Keepeth My Soul; as the music plays, please school leavers, take your favourite lovers or loves to the floor," Saffa went on. Bondawaa watched from the corner of his eye as his colleagues began to move to the floor in pairs. He turned his head around quickly and discovered that both Gbessay and Matu were eyeing him expectantly. Hot sweat began to run down his armpits, and his three-piece suit became too heavy for him.

"Please well-wishers, give them the floor. We want to see clearly who the heroes and heroines of this year's graduation dance are. As they occupy the floor, let us please clap for them." The clapping was thunderous; it almost brought the roof down. Rain began to drizzle, and cool breeze invaded the hall.

"Now there you are, Jesus is going to keep your souls, foul or fair," the MC concluded. The floor seemed expansive, magnifying every single dancer.

50

Bondawaa went to the floor alone, sluggard and leaned nervously on one of the pillars supporting the hall. "Jesus my brother, please help me; Jesus, please save me; Jesus Son of God, please come to my rescue," he prayed fervently, standing there dazed, waiting for Jesus to keep his soul. Jesus became incarnated in his friends. They came and made a barricade around him and brought Gbessay and put her right in the centre.

While Bondawaa and Gbessay were dancing, his friends made sure that no other woman penetrated through the circle they had formed around him. Matu made several attempts to break through, but became ashamed and went away crying, feeling utterly dejected.

CHAPTER SIX

The Decisive Meeting

Saffa had been deferring college for God knows how long. He had been teaching at Ndema Academy as a pupil teacher for the past five years. The trio (Bondawaa, Moisia and Lappia) fondly referred to him as the Resident Minister of Ndema. He was not very keen on women, but he loved booze. The only time when he did not booze was when he did not have money enough. However, Saffa was very friendly. He relied heavily on friendship and people. He had always used friendship to achieve diverse ends.

"If Saffa has not used friendship to find his way into college, why will I not use it to convince him to do so?" Bondawaa asked himself one day. Aside from the usual fun the trio had about Saffa's delay in going to college; it became Bondawaa's genuine concern every now and then to persuade him to do so.

Bondawaa knew Saffa's weakness very well, this young man! One evening, he invited him to a pub. He chose an isolated corner for the two of them. He put in an order, and quite a reasonable number of pints of beer were placed on the table by a good-looking schoolgirl who smiled at Saffa all the time she performed this chore.

"What are we celebrating?" Saffa asked in a joyous mood, licking his mouth playfully.

"Nothing really, I'm just trying to set the climate for a crucial brotherly dialogue," Bondawaa said, smiling broadly at him. He allowed a long silence to lapse before he spoke again. Saffa was just about to engage his second bottle when Bondawaa cleared his throat. Saffa smiled. He was a witty guy. He knew very well that Bondawaa was up to something but was waiting patiently for him to let the cat out of the bag.

"Saffa, how do you feel when we have already completed college and you are still in the classroom as a pupil teacher?" Bondawaa finally came out with the subject.

"I know you guys don't take me seriously. But who cares. Have I ever complained to any of you? As for book, I know it more than anyone of you three. I also have money more than the resources of all of you three put together. So why do you want to bother me?"

"It is difficult to advise someone older than you, but I'm strongly convinced that you need a university degree to boost your prestige and socio-economic status. You have the ability, so I'll not forgive you for wasting your own time, your wife's, and your poor children's," Bondawaa said a little firmly.

"Now, Bondawaa, if my children hunger in future, will you not feed them?" Saffa asked rather playfully.

"I will, but you have to lay a good foundation for them and that is what I want to help you do." A spell of silence dawned on them. The pretty schoolgirl appeared again suddenly and leaned on Saffa and began to ruffle his hair. He did not want her to encroach on their privacy for long. "Nothing will save you from getting a sound beating from me tomorrow if you do not do my assignment," he threatened. She ran away making faces at him.

53

When they left the pub that night, Saffa had resolved to go to college the following academic year.

When Saffa gained admission to the Arts Faculty in Bombay College, University of Simbeck, there was a great celebration. At about 10:00 pm on a Friday, as usual, the trio was sitting at the Liyah Bar drinking when a young man appeared, clutching at a travelling bag. He was drunk and worn-out, having walked seventeen miles to bring home to his wife, children, and friends – and in fact the whole township – news of this great achievement.

No sooner did he walk into the bar than he sat down, opened his bag, took out a giant bottle of dry gin and began to help himself to it. For the trio a behaviour such as that was not strange. Liyah, the only popular bar in Ngawobu, was the centre of humour and buffoonery. They had themselves occasionally contributed to the diverse comic scenarios that went on in the place.

The strange figure that had dramatically entered the bar was Saffa, but the trio missed him completely. He enjoyed the miss and continued to drink alone; first in a ceremonial way and later ravenously. "Only Saffa can drink dry gin as if drinking water or perhaps this is another Saffa," Lappia said. In the next ten seconds his suspicion was confirmed, the man began to sing:

> *Reticence*
> *Bush fowl reticence*
> *I am a secret society leader*
> *A lesser man should not tell my bathing place*

Reticence
Bush fowl reticence
If you were man enough
You could know where I bathe

Reticence
Bush fowl reticence
If you pay a hero's keepsake
You could know where I bathe

Reticence
Bush fowl reticence
If you were not too jealous
You could know where I bathe

Reticence
Bush fowl reticence
If you were not blinded by love
You could know where I bathe

Reticence
Bush fowl reticence
Do not be hoodwinked by love
And not know where I bathe

Soon the trio was standing around Saffa. "The bush fowl reticence" was Saffa's favourite song. It could not have been sung by any other person in the circumstances. But even as they stood round him, they still needed to be assured further if the fellow was really Saffa. He was, or pretended to be so drunk that

55

he could not even open his eyes properly. But when he smiled in their face, with the fine gap in his upper teeth, they all yelled out.

"But when did you come back from Gracetown, Saffa?" asked Lappia.

"I am just arriving, fellows, just arriving; I have not even been to my house yet."

"How did you come?" Moisia asked.

"I walked. What is seventeen miles? When I got to Kwabu there was not a single vehicle coming in this direction, so I walked. It took me only three hours!"

"What could have made you walk such a long distance, and at night?" Bondawaa enquired.

"I have made it, guys. I've easily succeeded in doing what you imbeciles could not. I have been admitted in Bombay College," Saffa told the trio, elated, and flashed his acceptance letter in their faces. "You better sit down and swallow some beers on me. Are there enough beers in here for these bloody fools?" Saffa asked. Now glowing with life, he took control of the bar and injected vitality in all those who were there.

He ordered that everyone at the bar should drink on him; stopped the pop music that was blaring from the musical set and led the trio in singing a Bundo song. If you saw him now, you would never believe it was the same man who had come in not too long ago. Everyone in the bar was now on his/her feet dancing in a circle round Saffa. Even the bar owner, a beautiful and stately looking woman, was in the circle that hemmed in on Saffa. Their voices cascaded through the serene air and jolted the hearts of some music lovers who were in their houses.

Very soon, the bar became too small a place to accommodate the merry makers. They danced in the open air in front of the bar for a brief while. But when a professional female singer offered to help Saffa lead the singing, and some indigenous musical instruments were being played to accompany the songs, it became an occasion for the entertainment of the whole town. As the elders would say, it became a pair of trousers with a band too big for the waist of a child.

"If an elder has blood to spill, he walks out of his house even after he had already gone to bed." Many slighted this proverbial saying when the group left the bar for the township. People came from all directions to join the dance: men, women and even children. It was now early in the morning and the place was already chilly. Saffa therefore bought locally distilled wine to keep his celebrants warm. As they danced, each house they visited, Saffa would make an elaborate speech on his admission. It would cover the faculty, subjects to be studied and their relevance to the job he would eventually get.

When he got the Bachelor of Arts degree, Saffa celebrated it in a way more dramatic than he did his admission to the college.

HAPTER SEVEN

Bondawaa goes to Gracetown

When Bondawaa decided to leave for Gracetown, Simbeck's capital city, in search of a job, he needed something to carry his clothes in. The night before he left, Bondawaa's mother called him into her bedroom. It was about 8:00 pm and Bondawaa had reserved this evening to say goodbye to his closest friends. He sat on the bed by her and looked over the important items in the room. There was the earthen pot, which they had often said cools water more than a refrigerator does; the twin's shrine, which the older family members fed once every year during the harvest season; and the soot-coloured mosquito net which had been hanging on this bed since Bondawaa became conscious of the world around him.

As Bondawaa counted the valuables in his mother's room, he began to feel sorry that he had to leave his community behind. This room had served him in various ways. He had always hidden away from his cousins in this room at night and re-joined them with his stomach bulging. In this room, Bondawaa's mother had often showered him with food, and imparted warnings against the evils of the new world. "*Ye* (mother), I wish I were able to fly from the city to this room and back each time I am in need," Bondawaa said to his mother. His mother stared at him for a moment and said, "I never knew you were a witch. But even if you are one, you should not fly over several

58

chiefdoms only to come and fill your tummy and then fly back. Who knows the hurdles you may encounter?" she asked. Silence fell upon the room, and in the quiet Bondawaa heard a mosquito buzzing close to his ear. As he tried to locate the tiny and yet dreaded insect, his mother's voice filled the void.

"I want you to carry your things in that portmanteau when you are leaving for Gracetown tomorrow. I have always treasured it greatly, because it's the most important thing your father bought for me upon my graduation from the Bundo society. But what can I treasure in this world more than you? You who sealed my relationship with your father but made me endure so much pain and indignities." She put her head down, hiding her tears from Bondawaa.

"You should not cry for your portmanteau, Njabu," he said trying to console his mother. "In fact, I have bought a nice carton in which I am going to carry my things tomorrow."

"You are wicked to say that I am crying because of the portmanteau. You are going away in search of a job in that evil city with no blood relation of yours to look after you," she protested. "Others started as Pupil Teachers or Native Administration Clerks here at home, and then went to college before going away finally from home. But you have decided to start far away in Gracetown where everyone is free to do what he or she likes; my forefathers, what a child!" Tears began to roll down her cheeks again. This time, she looked at her son straight in the face. Bondawaa was gripped by genuine sympathy for his mother whose worried and pathetic eyes were fixed on him.

"You should not love your child more than his future," Bondawaa said in his own defence. "You know I have had all my schooling here at home, from class one to form five. I need a change if I must make it in life," Bondawaa tried to explain to his mother the reason for moving to the city. Njabu held up Bondawaa's right hand and spat in his palm. "Press it on your forehead," she instructed.

He did accordingly. "I laboured for my parents and obeyed them. I would have divorced your father and married another man, but because of the respect and love I have for my parents I am with him today. Aside from that, I cannot afford to run away and leave you the children in a home run by another woman. Our people say that a mother hen should not jump over fire. I have had to endure indignities from your father. Some were done before your very eyes. Even when you were big enough to defend me, you could not dare. Our values will not allow you. I have continued to endure up to this very moment." She held her head in both hands and began to weep again. Bondawaa did not know if he should cry or not. He bit his lower lip hard, trying to control himself, but he could not. The tears flowed freely; tears of uncertainty mixed with sympathy for his mother. As she was llooking away, with her head now supported by her right hand, Njabu murmured, "Go to Gracetown tomorrow, I know you will prosper there. My blessing and the blessing of my parents will always be with you."

Before he left Ngawobu for Gracetown, Bondawaa's father had a one-on-one meeting with

60

him. This was the time his father confessed to him that he was now sick and was therefore not sure if he would be able to pay school fees for the other children again, Bondawaa's younger brothers and sisters. He insisted with the authority of a father that it was now Bondawaa's responsibility to ensure his younger brothers and sisters got higher education, even higher than what he had had. Bondawaa chuckled. "Why do you chuckle when I am talking to you?" his father flared up in anger. "You think all the money we have spent on you to gain this wealth of education was meant for your enjoyment alone, eh; and for the enjoyment of the educated wife, you would marry in future? Who in this family has ever had the opportunity of completing form five? I know that as a form five graduate, there is too many books in that head of yours. With my blessings and that of your mother, there is a good job awaiting you anywhere in this country, even in the white man's country. You will get it by a stroke of the pen," Bondawaa's father said confidently.

This time Bondawaa suppressed a giggle. His father was a stern person. Despite Bondawaa's age, if he had seen him laugh at him for the second time, particularly when he was already angry, he would have given him a hot slap. "Papa please, I have not got enough formal education yet. I need a university degree before I consider myself educated," he told his dad persuasively. He told Bondawaa that if he wanted to pursue any further education it would be purely at his own expense and that he should combine it with the cost of the education and other expenses of his younger brothers and sisters.

By the time Bondawaa left for Gracetown his father had five wives: Haku, Njabu, Lombeh, Nyambe, and Moinya in that order; and a total of fourteen children. Haku, the head-wife, had no child; Njabu, Bondawaa's mother, had five surviving children, Lombeh four children, Nyambe two children, and Moinya, the fifth, youngest, and his father's favourite, had produced three children and had the potential to produce even seven more.

CHAPTER EIGHT

Bondawaa in Gracetown

Once they entered the city, it took their minibus an unusually long time to get to its last station. This was because after every hundred yards or so, someone would reach his or her destination and ask the driver, through the driver's mate, to stop. So, the driver's mate announced two or three stops in advance to refresh the memories of the passengers: "Any Lab Lane; Grass Land; Banana Lane?" If a passenger wanted to alight at Lab Lane, for example, he would say "*Wan na Lab Lane*" (stop at Lab Lane) and the driver's mate would relay it to his *Bosman* (the driver), "*Go de fɔ Lab Lane*" and the driver would stop there for the passenger to alight.

Bondawaa did not want to alight anywhere except at Santana, the last station. He had been advised to board a taxi from there for No. 15 Cockroach Street if he wanted to save time and money. The many stops confused Bondawaa, particularly because he was coming to a city as big as this for the first time in his life.

As the bus drove through the rather endless city sprawled on either side of the road, he saw an extensive, lurching mountain border to the left and the sea to the right. In between, an army of people moved about like ants. The women were balancing all kinds of load on their heads, while the men carried weights on their shoulders twice as big as those carried by the

63

women. The traffic was quite heavy. It would move like a snail for a few seconds, come to a standstill for five or ten minutes, and then move again for another five minutes or so. Though he had become frustrated by the slow traffic, Bondawaa could not quite make up his mind to alight from the bus. The fear of getting lost in this gigantic city, often described as crime-infested, began to worry him.

Soon, Bondawaa's stomach began to rumble, and he could feel the poo trying to force its way down. Barely holding it in, he started to foul the ear in tight little bursts. Each time he emitted the gas; the woman seated next to him would ask if somebody had rotten fish on board the bus. The other passengers would sniff the air, quite to Bondawaa's embarrassment, to locate the source of the foul odour.

"Any Fakai Junction, Lamina Street Junction, Kanneh Street?" the apprentice asked, resuming his announcement of approaching stops. Out of shame and torment, and conscious that he was suffocating the other passengers with the putrid smell of the faeces that was already rubbing its nose on his briefs, Bondawaa told the apprentice he was getting off at Kanneh Street.

Bondawaa followed Kanneh Street leading towards Kongobay Road. He walked with his buttocks tightly clasped together, and in quick short strides. He held his portmanteau firmly, reading the names of the streets that branched off Kanneh Street to the left and the right. The significant thing about the portmanteau he was carrying was that it was two years his elder. It was one of the valuable things that his father bought for his mother when she was graduating from the Bundo society. It was now over twenty years old, but still new and not yet gone out of fashion.

The next street off Kanneh Street to the left was Cockroach Street. The massive heap of rubbish at its junction was the home of vultures. What was more, there were children rummaging in it too. It was in this garbage that Bondawaa saw the largest rat he had ever seen. It was as big as a groundhog, with bumpy legs that made it limp all over the placed. Amazingly, it was not bothered by the presence of the many people that plied this route.

Bondawaa had no problem locating Number 1–14, but number 15 was nowhere to be found. He could see numbers 16, 17, up to 20, but no 15. Maybe his nervousness and rustic fright were responsible for his inability to locate No. 15 Cockroach Street. "Jesus, son of David, please come to my aid," he began to pray quietly.

As if God was listening directly to this prayer and many others Bondawaa had offered before, a teenage boy walked up to him and asked, "Are you looking for somebody? You have been wandering up and down this street for a couple of minutes now." The boy was about fourteen years old, and looked like one of those boys who are homeless. His hair was shaggy, his clothes ripped and faded with a few patches here and there. His ribs were sticking out like most underfed children, and his body emitted a rancid smell, typical of one who had not had a bath for a whole week. He walked bare footed right in the heart of the capital city.

65

Aside from all this, he looked spirited as he stood there looking at Bondawaa with genuine concern.

"I am looking for ... emm ...e-e-ee, number 15 Cockroach Street," Bondawaa said hesitantly.

"Oh, please let me help carry your portmanteau. I live at number 15," the boy said, looking at Bondawaa confidently. "By the way are you looking for *Ngɔ* (reference to someone slightly your senior) Keifa? He has been expecting somebody from Ngawobu today," the boy continued. Even though the boy had named the person Bondawaa was looking for, and the town he was coming from that day, he still held on tightly to the portmanteau.

"Let us go, the portmanteau is not heavy," he lied. When they got to number 15, Keifa had not returned from work yet.

The occupants of the first floor of the rickety two-story wooden house, who Bondawaa found out to be the relations of Keifa, were very receptive. They offered him something to eat.

"Thanks very much, please let me rest a while first," he said politely. Bondawaa was famished, but he was not the least able to eat, for there was this excrement tormenting him. He had suppressed it, but the urge had returned, and was making his stomach rumble. Thank God, he was not letting out foul air anymore; otherwise Bondawaa would have been asked if he had some rotten fish in his portmanteau. He could not get himself to ask for the toilet. He still had the vague feeling that he was in the wrong place.

Keifa had his meals at number 15 Cockroach Street, but lived at number 1 Banana Street, just a few yards away. He led Bondawaa to see what was going to be their bedroom in Gracetown. The room was very small, and was in the basement, directly under the kitchen of a one-storey house. The occupants who lived on the floor above Keifa and Bondawaa used a three-stone open fire to cook. Each time they cooked the room of these two young men would be as hot as an oven. No sooner Keifa and Bondawaa entered the room than they began to sweat profusely. "The agama lizard does not sweat, the proverb goes, but not when it is in a room such as this one," Bondawaa remarked minutes after they had entered. The room had neither a chair nor a table. It had only a bed and Keifa's things were scattered all over the floor, some stacked in one of the corners.

"This room is ideal for all my visitors, because when they enter it, they have no alternative but to sit on the bed or on the floor," Keifa joked, laughing heartily.

Keifa directed Bondawaa to the latrine. It was a dug-out pit, shallow and already filled to the brim with faeces. There were also faeces littered all over the floor, and the walls were smeared with it. The floor was a pool of urine mingled with water people had used to clean themselves up after they had used the latrine. Bondawaa was gripped by violent nausea and began to throw up.

"Is this what I will be using every day?" he wondered as he reeled from the retching. He would not have dared use the latrine if his stomach was not bursting with poo trying to find its way out. The condition of the latrine was such that it was more convenient to banish half standing than squatting. When he left the latrine, Bondawaa asked for water to bathe to rid himself of the stench. But Jesus, the bathroom was equally filthy! His nausea heightened and his head began to spin.

When Bondawaa returned to their tiny bedroom, he began to throw up. "What the hell is this boast our brothers and sisters make about being in the city when they return to the provinces, with all this filth, heat and congestion that I have been confronted with?" he asked Keifa.

"When a presenter says on our national broadcasting service in the morning 'This is Gracetown', he or she is reminding us of the filth, overcrowding, crime, prostitution, pickpocketing, robbery and what have you. This is just the beginning of your initiation into city life. If you keep on throwing up, you will pull out all your entrails before long. Welcome to the city, my brother", Keifa teased Bondawaa, almost choking with laughter.

CHAPTER NINE

Bondawaa's Dream

The coffin had just been lowered into the grave after a series of fitful dirges. The most mournful was the one by Bondawaa's mother. When she opened her mouth to sing, it was seconds before the words came out. They were scarcely audible. She trembled as she sang, and her eyes were as red as fire at dusk.

Depart we all must
From this harrowing world
But a full-grown male child
Before parents
Is like putting out fire
From a family hearth
On harsh harmattan morning
My nipples will forever gather mold
Never again to suckle a baby
When life departs from me
A permanent wayfarer
My destitute spirit shall be too
Scared to face her forefathers in the bowels of the earth
Where the impoverished are relieved of their burdens forever

Njabu's dirge gripped the hearts of many. She swooned and fell by the graveside. When the coffin had been covered firmly in the mud and everybody had

69

departed, the cemetery was soon enveloped in a forest chorus. Frogs were croaking, the crickets chirping, and the birds sang melodious tunes. As the sun disappeared into the bowels of the horizon, night took full control, and the cemetery became a mass of darkness. Hunger was gnawing at Bondawaa, and he felt overcome by loneliness. He tried to pray several times, but his lips did not move. Words failed him, as he lay there helpless, trying to imagine things. There was a sudden tremor, the grave expanded and Bondawaa sat up in what now looked like a dining room. An aroma of celestial perfume filled the surrounding. Suddenly, there emerged a woman with a piece of cotton cloth tied over her breast. She was very dark, with an imposing personality. This exquisite work of nature stood away, looking at Bondawaa with amusement.

"*Maa* (grandmother), I am hungry," Bondawaa said unconsciously.

"I am here to feed you, my grandchild," she said and beckoned to him to move closer. Bondawaa rose feeling spent. As he was walking up to her, with his legs knocking against each other, she undid the knot of the lappa carefully, held out her right breast, squeezed its nipple and left the milk to run freely.

"Your body is devoid of the milk of love for your kith and kin; that is the hunger that is biting deep into your guts and soul, and into those of your generation," she said, still holding her breast.

"How can you feed an adult on your breast milk?" Bondawaa queried with a cloud of doubt on his face.

"Those of you reared on foreign milk should go back and suckle your mothers' breast milk, no matter

70

how old you are. I say it is only your mothers' breast milk that will make you know yourselves and your people better," the old woman said.

"I cannot understand this kind of practice," Bondawaa said, rather defiantly.

"You will not because you have not got enough of your mother's milk running in your system," she said and let out a laugh that vibrated and reverberated in the underground room.

"Please don't go, I am starving", Bondawaa yelled out to her as she turned round and was about to depart.

The milk was fresh, cool, and resuscitating. It took away Bondawaa's hunger and restored in him peace of mind, love, and courage. As soon as she disappeared, he was once more shrouded by darkness. The first chorus had been replaced. It was now a low pitch of baritones. The players were owls, vampires, and bullfrogs. He became extremely afraid, and his blood went cold. For the second time Bondawaa thought of praying; but his lips again would not move. Tears welled up in his eyes like rain and ran down his cheeks. Just then, a heavy storm with thunder and lightning broke out followed by torrential rain. It rained as if the sky had burst open. The cemetery became one mass of water, and the flood washed Bondawaa away. As he swam and looked for the nearest land, he saw a boat heading in his direction, "A rescuer or a cannibal?" Bondawaa asked himself. As the boat approached, he thought of the *Kongobay* (a submarine made locally), used by cannibals to catch fishermen.

"God, am I going to die twice?" he yelled. The nearer the boat drew to him, the more Bondawaa became convinced that he knew the lone passenger on board. The passenger was bearded and grey and was draped with an embroidered country cloth robe. The boat was within reach now, and Bondawaa recognized his late grandfather, "*Maada* (granddad)!" he shouted with joy and relief. He gripped the rim of the boat firmly as he struggled to get on board. His granddad held him by both hands and hauled him into the boat. He stood over Bondawaa for some five minutes, as he lay flat on his stomach on the floor of the boat, throwing up gallons of water he had gulped while trying to swim.

"I am happy that you were able to hold out for that long, and bravely too. I can see that you are now both physically and mentally prepared for the great task ahead of you," his granddad said as soon as Bondawaa sat up.

"Task? I have now left it behind me. The wailing was incessant when I left."

"Nothing like that, it was merely a transition process meant to prepare you for your new role."
"Transition?"

"Yes, you are a fighter. With the blood of your great granddad running in your veins, and the fresh milk of your great grandmother transfused into you, you are sure to put up an impressive fight."

"I need his sword as well," Bondawaa said, smiling assuredly.

"You will fail woefully if you use it. What you need is a tactful use of the mixture of his blood, the

72

milk of your great-grandmother, and the new ways you have acquired from school. Too much of anyone will create an imbalance."

As they got closer to the shore his granddad stood up in the boat looking ahead. Though completely grey, the old man was still the same man Bondawaa had known strong, defiant, and light-hearted. As soon as the boat berthed, Bondawaa's granddad held him by the hand and off they went. Sprawled before them was vast expanse of grassland. The wind was gentle, rustling through the blades. A flock of cattle egrets flew before them, with sunrays buffeting them as they went. Bondawaa thought that cattle egrets were the spirits of cattle, especially cows. When they were little boys, they were told that egrets were spirits, that the cattle do not see egrets at all even when they fly in front of them or sit on their backs. Now in this other world, they fly serenely. How mysterious, Bondawaa thought. His granddad stopped suddenly and turned.

"Your life in Gracetown is not going to be easy. It is going to be full of challenges. You will see people kill others. People will lie, steal, cheat, profiteer, they will commit adultery and become prostitutes, all in the name of money. You will see poverty amid plenty. You will see people deny their parents and relations in the quest for wealth. You must not fall victim to these vices," his granddad said and paused.

"I have already begun to witness some of them during the few days I have been there. The whole place reeks of corruption."

"I am worried that you may become corrupt."

"I will be an observer."

"An observer, when will there ever be a challenger?" the old man almost growled at Bondawaa. His granddad eyed him so sternly that he felt helpless and wanted to cry.

"But Granddad, how can…"

"You might be a lone fighter, I know. But you will make some impact if you fight hard" the old man said and turned away from him. As Bondawaa cast his eyes in the other direction, he saw Gracetown sprawled before him, gleaming in the setting sun. He woke up sweating profusely.

CHAPTER TEN

Saffa's Letter from Ngawobu

A month later Bondawaa was sitting in front of No. 1 Banana Street early in the morning, brooding over his slim chances of ever getting a job. He had no training certificates, or connections in high places. A mail carrier stopped in front of him, held out a letter and asked, "Do you know if a Bondawaa Ndoma lives here?" pointing at the inscription of Number One on the gate post.

"I am called by that name," he said. The mail carrier gave him the letter and asked if he was a newcomer to the area. That was Bondawaa's first letter in Gracetown. He became eager, thinking that it was a reply to one of the dozens of application letters he had sent out in search of employment. The letter was not typed, and the handwriting was familiar. "This must be from Saffa at Ngawobu," he guessed. The letter was to inform Bondawaa that the girl he had impregnated while they were in form five had given birth to a bouncing baby girl.

"Please come and see your first fruit, and come like a man," the letter concluded.

"Beans don't bear well when planted by someone whose fingers are intact," he muttered to himself. "Bloody fool! Who told you the child is mine?" He cursed the author light-heartedly, feeling somewhat elated. The pregnancy had haunted him throughout his preparations for the General Certificate of Education Ordinary Level (GCE O'Level) examinations.

In those days, contraceptives were rare. Bondawaa was not sure whether he should own up to the pregnancy or not.

In the traditional African society, a child is wealth. Therefore, Bondawaa's mother vowed to curse him if he denied responsibility for the pregnancy.

"You know I have given birth to nine children and only five have survived. All five of them are males, no daughter! What are my chances of getting at least a grand daughter if you, the first fruit of my womb, are to start by denying responsibility for pregnancy?" Njabu asked in rage.

Having nursed the contents of Saffa's letter for the better part of that day, Bondawaa went to a distant relation in the evening for help and advice. He went there with his heart in his mouth because this uncle was well known for teasing. He was an employee of the Ministry of Finance, the first crop of young people from Ngawobu chiefdom to get a university degree from the country's highest and oldest institution of learning. Among those with university degrees in Ngawobu chiefdom, he rated himself as number one, though other people held a different view. In gatherings, he would always praise his Bachelor of Science in Accounting degree, the first such achievement in Ngawobu chiefdom.

When Bondawaa got to his uncle's place, the man from the Ministry of Finance ordered his houseboy to serve him a coke without asking which drink he wanted, "Please don't give him a glass, he does not know how to drink from it," his uncle said laughing at Bondawaa's discomfort. As Bondawaa sipped the coke, his uncle asked, "What are you doing in Gracetown?"

"In search of a job, sir," Bondawaa answered.

"How many pairs of shoes do you have?" his uncle asked, laughing jovially.

"Just one, sir," he answered, feeling uneasy.

"I advise you to send to your parents for another pair or two, to be better prepared for the task of job-hunting.

"Thank you for that advice, sir," Bondawaa said weakly and faked a smile.

CHAPTER ELEVEN

Gracetown at Night

Keifa returned from work at midnight one day and complained of hunger. "I want to eat a loaf of bread, hot and straight from the oven. Please accompany me to the nearest bakery, Bondawaa," he said. Bondawaa grew pale; the idea of being arrested and locked up in an overcrowded and unsanitary dungeon of a cell crossed his mind.

"You know it is not safe to be on the street by now", he told Keifa, looking at his watch.

"In the city you should not be too much of a coward. If you do you will be target," Keifa said, laughing at Bondawaa.

Bondawaa needed a job very badly and did not want to languish in somebody's cell for loitering. But he hated being called a coward, so he got up and they left.

The bakery was three-streets up from where they lived on Banana Street. Just after they crossed the first street, they bumped into a pair of policemen on patrol. They were a special class of police known as the National Protection Division (NPD). They pointed their rifles at Keifa and Bondawaa, set them at half cock: "*If yu muf wi ko sut* (if you move, we will shoot)," they said in heavily accented Krio. The danger about these special police force was that most of them were illiterate and could not even speak Krio. They often said that they knew only the gun, not book.

They walked up to Keifa and Bondawaa with their guns pointed and asked why they were loitering when they knew that they were not supposed to be on the street by that time. From the moment they set eyes on the police, Bondawaa began racking his brain to come up with a reason for them being on the street after 11 pm, which marked the start of curfew.

Suddenly he heard people singing not too far away. He told the police that they were coming from the wake, and that they had run out of bread and were running to the near-by bakery for more loaves. The police asked for some cash and warned Bondawaa and Keifa about meeting them again when they returned.

Every morning, the police at the various Gracetown stations, collected huge sums of money from people who came to bail out their family members who had been jailed for so-called loitering. Those who had money on them when they were arrested for loitering settled the matter with the police there and then to avoid going to jail. There were also the "untouchables" in Gracetown, who could loiter and rabble rouse for the whole night, but the law would look at them with a kindly eye.

79

CHAPTER TWELVE

Jobless in Gracetown

Bondawaa had now spent three months in Graceland without a job. He sat in an open space in front of No. 1 Banana Street and started thinking about the state of his country. This was the era when new words such as *monitocracy* and *connectocracy* were creeping in. "Where will all of this lead us to?" he wondered as he rose and began to move. By the time he crossed three streets, he realized that he was wandering aimlessly and thinking aloud. "What, does it mean now that in Simbeck one has to have connections in high places before you get a job?"

Incompetent people filled important offices, because they had the right connections, and competent people who did not have the right connections were left to suffer or work under the incompetent. There were many square pegs in round holes. This incompetent lot was always quick to assert their importance. "Do you know who I am?" they would ask when they felt confronted. Some officials, especially in government ministries and agencies were not only incompetent, but also got away with it.

Government workers would go to work at 10:00 am, break for lunch at noon and then come back to work at 2:00 pm. Even the few hours they spent at work they would use on long telephone conversations. The public bribed Civil servants so files could move through the bureaucratic process. Files got lost in government offices, only to reappear after palms had been greased. In Simbeck, monitocracy outweighed connectocracy. Business cards, family ties and other connections had lost the value they once had. If you went to somebody's office with a business card, he would tell you his family does not feed on complimentary cards. Everything was about cash. Jobs were bought. The more money you were ready to pay, the better your chances were of getting a good job or admission in some educational institutions, especially tertiary ones. Scholarships were no longer won by your qualifications. Neither were promotions in the public service.

As an unemployed person in a country such as Simbeck was, Bondawaa's position was precarious. He felt like an errand boy who had to walk several miles to take food to a starving family. How far will he get before sunset? What will happen to the starving people?

CHAPTER THIRTEEN

A Job Offer

It was now October, and the rainy season had just ended. The rains had washed away the dust from all the corrugated roofs in Gracetown and exposed the rust. Some of the roofs were real eyesores but the air was fresh. The rains had also shifted the clogged-up sewage in the gutters. The rays of the morning sun hit Bondawaa aggressively in the face. As he raised his head up, he saw that it was a sparkling morning. The sky was covered with a carpet of white and blue downy cloud, twinkling in the early dry season sunlight. A hawk circled hundreds of feet in the air.

Piima and Bondawaa had been discussing the illness of the latter's father when a messenger arrived with a letter from the Education Office of Gracetown City Council. He asked Bondawaa to sign the way-book before he could give it to him. He signed it promptly. The interview for the position of Assistant Teacher at one of the Gracetown City Council primary schools was four days ahead. Bondawaa's dilemma was whether to attend it before going to see his sick father.

He discussed his dilemma with Keifa who advised him to wait until after the interview. "You can always go and see your sick father, but there is only one date set for the interview," he advised.

Bondawaa appeared in the reception room of Gracetown City Council Education Office at 8:00 am for an interview scheduled for 9:00 am. The receptionist was a frail-looking woman. She was hostile both in appearance and manners. She was eating a loaf of bread stuffed with fried fish and pancake when Bondawaa walked into her office. She did not talk to any of the interviewees who had entered whilst she was eating, until she had finished.

Her first utterance was "Why are you invading my office, you people?" She probably meant it as a joke, but for Bondawaa, she showed a lack of courtesy by not inviting them to the meal, even if half-heartedly. Bondawaa took in his surroundings. The office had a typewriter and a telephone, plus four dining chairs, one of which had only three legs. The telephone receiver and the typewriter were some twenty years older than the receptionist. Yet, she sat behind them ostentatiously, treating people with contempt. They had lined up some benches along the wall for the interviewees to sit on. The walls looked as if they had not been painted in years. The ceiling had strands of spider webs and the floor had holes here and there, because damaged tiles had been removed.

The interviewers arrived at 10:00 am, exactly one hour late. From the way they walked in one could guess that coming late to that office was a norm. They walked past the interviewees smiling and disappeared into a room on the lefthand corner of the reception desk and shut the door behind them loudly.

"Waiyo Amao", they called out the first name behind the locked door. Every one of the interviewees became very alert.

"They are going in alphabetical order. I will be interviewed after several candidates," Bondawaa muttered. However, he was the third person to be called. While he was waiting, a lot of thoughts crossed his mind. "I have no connections, I have not met any of the interviewers personally, and how am I going to get this job?" With this train of thoughts racing through his mind, Bondawaa was called in. He entered panic-stricken and shaking. The interviewers laughed and gave him some time to catch his breath.

"Mr. Ndoma, why do you want to teach?" one of the interviewers asked.

"Because I have no other job to do," he answered frankly.

"Does that mean you want to use teaching as a last resort?" another question was fired at him.

"That's right," he answered.

"Please learn to say yes sir or madam," he was reprimanded.

"Yes sir, madam", he said, confused. Bondawaa became even more nervous and began to shiver.

"Now Mr. Ndoma, I can see that you have five GCE 'O' level passes and still you want to teach. Why don't you go to college and pursue a degree course?" the Education Officer asked him.

"It is because my parents are poor. I must work to pay school fees for my younger brothers and sisters, particularly the one who is now in form four. My father is almost an invalid."

"Mr. Ndoma, which part of Simbeck do you come from?" "Ngawobu in the eastern province," he lied.

"But you have both cash crops and diamonds in the eastern province."

84

"Yes, but our family land has no diamonds, and my father did not grow any cash crops."

"Suppose we employ you, which class would you like to teach?"

"Preferably class seven, but I will not mind six or five." "If not?"

"I will endeavour to teach class four or class three; classes two and one will not benefit much from my teaching."

"Thank you, Mr. Ndoma, it has been a lot of fun talking to you. From today onwards count on me as your "girlfriend", and goodbye," an elderly lady interviewer said. He left the room with mixed feelings.

CHAPTER FOURTEEN

Back in Ngawobu before South-Day

When Bondawaa got to Ngawobu his father had just been discharged from the hospital. What ailed him was not quite clear to the doctors. They had, however, advised him to stop smoking and drinking. There was already a strong rumour among family members, neighbours, and friends that his father had been bewitched. "Salobu Hospital, the most renowned in the whole country, cannot diagnose what is wrong with the man, and yet he is ill. Isn't that strange? Can you now see the power of witchcraft and the black man's juju?" Bondawaa's mother told him shortly after he had arrived.

Back at home after some time in the crowded slums of Gracetown city; Bondawaa appreciated the freshness of the air, and the naturalness of rural life. He loved the aroma of the wildflowers at the break of dawn and at sunset, the music of birds. Rural people were simple; the foods were organic, and the women were effortlessly beautiful. They did not paint their lips, wear wigs, or bleach their skin, but they were beautiful. Indeed, the world of the city contrasted sharply with that of his rural community.

When he got back to Gracetown, Bondawaa found a letter asking him to report to the Gracetown City Council doctor for a medical test. The test was, in his opinion, obscene! A stern-looking retired medico told him to undress as soon as he entered the surgery.

Bondawaa removed his shoes, trousers, and shirt. The doctor looked him over with an owlish eye and asked growlingly, "Were you born with socks and briefs on?" Bondawaa shuddered. "Sorry sir, I did not know I had to remove everything," he said, embarrassed.

The doctor felt his pulse, his heartbeat, examined his eyes, ears, nostril and bunghole. He took hold of his prick and began to squeeze it.

"Does it hurt?" he asked.

"No sir," he answered. Soon Bondawaa began to put on his clothes. "This is a lot of humiliation for a teaching job," he thought as he walked out of the surgery. He recalled a similar experience that he had when he was circumcised several years ago.

A week after the medical test, the same messenger who brought the interview letter came to Bondawaa's house at about 11:00 am and asked him to report at the Gracetown City Council Education Office.

"Did they send my taxi fare with you?" he asked the messenger excitedly.

"*Bɔs, dat na fɔ yu yone gud* (boss, it is for your own good)," the messenger said as he walked away. Bondawaa dressed hurriedly and boarded a taxi for the office. When he got there, the Education Officer asked whether he was interested in the job or not, as his appointment letter had been lying in his office for a week. "What, does it mean that I had been appointed before the officious-looking old doctor stripped me naked?" he asked himself.

From the Education Officer's office, he went straight to the Head Teacher of the afternoon shift of

South-Day Municipal Primary School and presented his appointment letter to her. The Head Teacher was a very pleasant-looking woman in her early fifties. They had already conducted devotion when Bondawaa got to the school and pupils in the other classes had started their first lessons.

"I am very pleased to have you on my staff, Mr. Ndoma. Class seven A has been without a teacher since their teacher went to college nearly three weeks ago. You look so young and inexperienced, straight from school?" the Head Teacher asked.

"Yes, Ma."

"The children will enjoy learning from you. Please come and meet your class," she led the way. They were soon upstairs, standing in front of a class of forty-one pupils. Most of them were between the ages of 11 and 13 years. The few provincial children who were there had official ages between 13 and 15 years. She introduced Bondawaa to the class and left. He stood in front of the children not knowing exactly what to do. His first job came with a chance to pour knowledge into the heads of young boys and girls. They sat there, looking at him expectantly. He did not know where to start. He opened his mouth several times, but no audible word came out. "Oh, being a teacher is such a difficult task," he thought.

CHAPTER FIFTEEN

The Reunion

One afternoon Bondawaa was having a beer at a kiosk when a little boy got cheeky with him. He grew very angry not so much because of the boy's misdemeanour but because he was sitting there drinking away the few Dabras he had, as if he was one of those civil servants grown fat on government coffers. He had taken to occasional drinking to cool off the tension that kept building in his head because he worried so much about every little thing. "I will beat you and the person that put you in charge of this kiosk," Bondawaa told the boy.

A woman came to the kiosk and the boy told her what Bondawaa had said. As the boy was giving his message to her, Bondawaa glanced in their direction and saw a very familiar face, one that he had known three years or so back. He gulped the beer quickly and walked away. "If this is Matu, this is the wrong place for her to find me in Gracetown." He did not feel like going back home at that moment. He went to another kiosk a couple of yards away. As he sat there quietly burying his thoughts deep in beers, he saw the same woman coming towards him. She had changed her dress and was looking much prettier than he saw her just recently. He got up, left his beer on the table, and started to walk away. "Young man, please wait a minute," the lady halted him. He ran and the lady ran

89

after him. "If you don't stop, I will shout thief, and the mob will fall on you," she threatened.

Bondawaa stopped, looking at the lady as she walked hurriedly to him. "Has she taken this kid's message that seriously; but wait a minute, is this Matu or her resemblance? Why is she chasing me? Has she been wronged by someone that I resemble? Surely this is a mistaken identity. I am sure this is not Matu; this lady is much fresher and more beautiful. Oh God, what trouble have I fetched for myself this evening?" All these thoughts ran through Bondawaa's mind in a few seconds. The lady grabbed him by the hand. "Follow me," she commanded. He followed her meekly. They were now at her kiosk and Bondawaa was looking at her, confused.

"Bondawaa, now I know that you are a beast, ungrateful and unloving. When you jinxed and humiliated me at your graduation dance, I blamed myself of being at fault, and a foolish woman with no heart and pride. But now I know that I was wrong to think that way. You are an ingrate," Matu went on in a tirade. Bondawaa covered his face with both hands. "You are made offensively arrogant by your youthful handsomeness. You always arrogantly wait for women to tell you they love you. How many times do you want me to tell you I love you? I am sure you do not have any more love left in your heart for me. You only want to show off; to grab a God-sent opportunity to punish me, but I will not allow you," she went on as Bondawaa looked at her, dumbfounded.

"If I were you, I would react in the same way. But you know that true love does not act rashly, complain or revenge."

"I have said what I felt about your behaviour, now come and have some beers on me. Feel free; I am Matu, the same woman you met in the open field some time ago at Ngawobu."

As Bondawaa sat at her kiosk drinking slowly, he was not sure if it was in his good interest to hook up with Matu again.

****

The next evening when Bondawaa was at Matu's drinking half-heartedly, an off-white Mercedes Benz car pulled up and parked close to the kiosk. A corpulent middle-aged man emerged from it with a voluminous cigar stuck to his lips and started to wriggle towards them like a palm-maggot. Matu wasted no time in introducing Bondawaa to the man as her first cousin just come from Ngawobu. That night, he drank a lot of beer courtesy of the grotesquely obese man.

After the man had left the kiosk, Bondawaa stood up feeling dazed and looking far into space. It was a dry season night. The sky was azure and densely studded with stars. Far in the horizon the sky and the sea were in firm embrace. They formed a thick bluish mass. He longed to reach them, to get enmeshed in their complex embrace and form one solid peaceful union.

"If I tell you he is my uncle, will you believe?" Matu asked Bondawaa laughing mischievously.

"Why not, I mean he is old enough to even be your father. The only problem is that your cousin and your uncle do not know each other," he reacted rather sarcastically.

"I know you are being jealous. But I think there is no need for that. I love him only for his money," she said. He said that he did not care if Matu became the third or fourth wife of his own uncle or not.

Matu and Bondawaa left the kiosk together and strolled down Virgin Road without saying a word to each other. As they lay in bed that night, Matu felt obliged to explain to Bondawaa her relationship with the Benz man.

"My business in Kwabu failed after too many people took to selling the same commodity, drinks. But even before that I had been missing you very badly, so I went to Ngawobu to get even a glimpse of you, though I did not know how you would receive me. In Ngawobu, I was told you had left for Gracetown a year ago. When I returned to Kwabu, I made up my mind one day to go in search of you. In Gracetown I searched for you for good two months before I ran into Mr. Njagbai. I had no choice; I did not only need financial support, but somebody I could talk to in confidence. I mean somebody I could relate to." Bondawaa grunted, cleared his throat, and said jokingly, "And someone who will suffocate you with heavy nicotine smell".

There was some noise filtering into the room from a distance. People were knocking empty milk cans against each other, shouting and cursing. They were trying to drive away a supposed human boar-constrictor that they say swallow their children when they are asleep. Back in Kobabu, Bondawaa's mother and many other women had allegedly lost their children to the said human boar-constrictor and witches. Bondawaa was wondering whether human boar-constrictors and witches could exist in cities as huge as Gracetown.

"As our relationship progressed, Mr. Njagbai rented a self-contained flat for me, the very one we are now in, and also gave me twelve thousand Dabras to run the kiosk," Matu resumed the narrative. Bondawaa buried his head in the pillow and kept silent, more attentive now to the noise coming from outside than to her. "In addition to all that I have told you, he gives me two thousand Dabras every fortnight for my maintenance," she continued. Bondawaa still lay silent.

"Are you sleeping?" she asked.

"No, I'm just wondering where civil servants get all the money from to spend lavishly on women who are not their lawful wives, when their wages are small, and there are some of us who cannot even afford a square meal per day," he said rather restlessly. Matu told Bondawaa that Mr. Njagbai had a countless number of girlfriends, and that there were some for whom he had even bought cars and built mansions. "He will soon build my own house and buy my own car, a Mercedes Benz 300. I have got him to sign cheques for both, which are now in my custody," she told Bondawaa proudly with no remorse at all.

That night Bondawaa slept very little. "When will I ever get enough money, some of which I can spend on girlfriends, numerous girlfriends at that?" He kept on asking himself the same question until he started to cry in his sleep. In fact, he was already amid a dream in which he was told that his father had died back at home. "O, they are waiting for me, the first child, to go and head the funeral ceremonies of my father. But how will I go, being just employed and have yet to receive my first salary," he was wailing fitfully when Matu woke him up and said that he was crying in his sleep.

CHAPTER SIXTEEN

Working Life

Life in South-Day Municipal School was agreeable. Teaching was now fun for Bondawaa. There were a lot of young teachers on the staff. Some were straight from college, others straight from school trying to matriculate for college. The school was one of the largest, if not the largest, primary school in the whole of Gracetown. It was a huge U-shaped structure consisting of twelve classrooms on the top floor and eleven on the ground floor. It was run in two shifts, morning, and afternoon. The morning shift comprised class one to three and ran from 8:00 am to 12:00 noon. The afternoon session was made up of class four to seven and it started at 12:30 pm and ended at 5:30 pm.

Teaching at South-Day continued to interest Bondawaa. Most of the pupils were very intelligent and eager to learn. Added to this, the Head Teacher gave tremendous encouragement to her staff. In addition to her fine administration, there were two teachers on the staff who made life in South-Day afternoon shift entertaining and worth remembering. Messrs Faze and Kessy kept life at South-Day bustling. The children chanted their names wherever they passed. They were the stars of the school.

Mr. Kessy was a retired Head Teacher on his second inning. To him life did not mean much again. He had at that time attained, in his own little way, all that he wanted. He went back to the classroom only to

95

while away time. He was a tall, bulky man, very dark and partially bald with ample grey strands in his hair and beard. Despite his bulk and age, he was very harmonious. His playmate of the day was a teacher he found looking cross and dejected. He had a reputation for getting people out of their state of sadness into one of joy and peace. These qualities made him a very useful member of staff. He made the other teachers forget their worries, at least for a while. He had a good sense of humour, cracked jokes, and told stories. Every day when he went to school, he would write some work on the chalkboard for the pupils to do and would then move from class-to-class cracking jokes with his colleagues. If you do not want him to spend much time in your class, you should smile broadly as soon as you see him, he will then quickly leave your class.

One day, Bondawaa went to Mr. Kessy's class in search of a piece of chalk. He had been going through an exercise with his class. The subject was English Sentence, Pattern and Structure (ESPS). The topic was Verbs (Action Words). He had written some verbs on the chalkboard and was demonstrating their actions for the pupils to tell him what he was doing. The lesson went on like this:

TEACHER: Class, what am I doing?
CLASS: You are walking.
TEACHER: Again.
CLASS: You are walking.
TEACHER: Class, what am I doing?
CLASS: You are writing.
TEACHER: Again.

CLASS: You are writing.
TEACHER: Class, what am I doing?
CLASS: You are sitting.
TEACHER: Again.
CLASS: You are sitting.
TEACHER: Again.
CLASS: You are sleeping.
TEACHER: Again.
CLASS: You are sleeping.

By the time Bondawaa got to the entrance of Mr. Kessy's class, he was sleeping, and the pupils were making fun of him. "You are sleeping, you are sleeping," and they kept on singing, "You are sleeping" and jumping about the class. But poor man, each time he got woken up by the pupils' noise he would say "Again" and go back to sleep; and the pupils would intensify their sing-song response of "You are sleeping." This mimicry went on for a while before the pupils saw Bondawaa at the entrance of their classroom. At once they began to say, "You are sitting." This became a common joke in the afternoon session of South-Day.

Mr. Faze was a young untrained and unqualified teacher (UU) who had taught in South-Day for a couple of years before Bondawaa joined the staff. He was very energetic, hardworking, and very intelligent. At times Bondawaa wondered why Mr. Faze should not go to college and upgrade himself.

Invariably, Mr. Faze was too playful and carefree. Bondawaa began to understand why he and Mr. Kessy made such a very good pair. Once at a staff meeting, held for the purpose of crosschecking her teachers' records, the Head Teacher asked each member of staff to indicate his or her full name and qualifications. When his turn came Mr. Faze said that he was QBE. Even the Head Teacher did not know what his qualification meant until he said, "Qualified by Experience." It was great fun that day, some of the teachers laughed their sides out. In those days qualified teachers were hard to come by. The most qualified were those with the Teachers Certificate (TC) and in most primary schools one would count them on the fingers. The rest either had the Teachers Elementary Certificate (TEC) or nothing at all.

One afternoon Messrs. Kessy and Faze were the masters in charge of devotion. Mr. Kessy had come to school on time and was going through a series of warming-up exercises with the pupils when Mr. Faze joined him, sweating profusely and breathless. "School, now jump, everybody!" he interrupted Mr. Kessy with a counter instruction to the pupils. Soon there was chaos. The two teachers were in firm grip now and were whirling round. They landed on the ground with Mr. Faze on top, right in front of the pupils. Tension and embarrassment loomed large in the air. But when both got up laughing and shook hands, the whole school roared with excitement and clapped riotously for them. For most of the staff it was a very expensive joke; the kind that would eat away the meagre prestige left for the schoolteacher. The fact that they got away with their infantile prank was a relief to all the teachers.

It was when Bondawaa received his first pay packet that he realized the enormity of his task, and how ill prepared he was for it. His dream of a good life and bringing light to the budding generation of the Ndoma family through formal education appeared to be impossible. After he had paid his contribution for feeding and rent, sent school fees and other charges for his brother who was in secondary school, the school fees for those in primary school, and an allowance for his child, he had almost nothing left for clothing and pocket money for himself. Tears clouded his eyes and began to rain down his cheeks. Behind this cloud of melancholy stood the image of Bondawaa's granddad smiling at him reassuringly. He smiled back.

Bondawaa went to the kiosk that evening and asked Matu to drink some beers on him. She laughed and said, "I know you've been paid your first salary today, but that does not mean that you should float me in beer. You have a lot to do with that meagre salary of yours. Why can't you sit down and drink on me instead?" Matu was inexplicably kind to Bondawaa. At times he felt affronted by some of her kind gestures.

While Bondawaa was apportioning his salary and grumbling to himself one day, Keifa entered the room and stood over him unnoticed. "You would have been saved all this trouble if you had gone ahead to do the sixth form course as I had advised." Bondawaa started when Keifa talked.

"You know why I turned your advice down. I would have had a scholarship, but it would have been far inadequate for the financial requirements of that course. Where would I have found the additional funding from? Whatever problem I must go through now, I have no solution to, other than teaching. I will do it for only two years after which I will go to college," Bondawaa justified his decision.

"Knowing our parents as I do, these responsibilities now rest on your head permanently. How will you handle them when you are in college?" Keifa asked. Bondawaa's blood pressure was raised considerably by this question. It was only then it dawned on him that these problems were tenacious; and not only that, but also that they would multiply with time.

"Let us not cross that bridge now when we are two years from it," he told Keifa.

Their room in Gracetown was now accommodating five people, despite its size. This was creating a host of social problems for them. Aside from the fact that three people shared the same bed, two males and one female, and two on the floor, there was hardly a place left in the room for them to keep their cooking utensils. Rita had come to join her boyfriend, Keifa; Teddy had come from up country to do sixth form and had nowhere to stay; Martha, the girlfriend of Teddy, had also come to Gracetown to complete her Teachers Certificate course and preferred to stay with Teddy, since the college was non-residential – even if she slept on the floor.

Keifa and Rita became lovers when he was in form four at Ngawobu High. Then Rita was a student at Makpoima Women Teachers College. During the vacations when Rita would come to Ngawobu, she and

Keifa would always be found together. People used to refer to them as the inseparable. They went to church together, to the dancing hall, to the river to bathe – everywhere. Rita was smallish, round-faced, had squinted eyes and dark skin with long hair. She was very kind, but sometimes haughty.

Martha was a tall and stout woman, in every respect not Teddy's equal. Martha had a chronic sinusitis. Each time the attack came on her she would avoid everybody, even Teddy, and would behave slightly abnormally. So, they used to call her the lunatic. Teddy was such a nice fellow, not easily angered by anything. He loved booze and fun. Their situation was an easy climate for promiscuity, three full-grown men and two adult women sharing the same room. At night they would put out the light, and the whole room would become the home of darkness. How could a woman know, in a situation such as that, which man was touching her?

Bondawaa was the odd male in the group. What a threat he could have been to both Keifa and Teddy if he were the womanizing type. But he had an uncanny indifference to women, more so towards Rita and Martha. His indifference was always the topic of discourse each time he was left alone with their two ladies. In fact, it developed to an embarrassing state in that the topic was brought up not only when Keifa and Teddy were around, but even in the presence of other friends. For Rita and Martha, Bondawaa was a she-man, a eunuch put in charge of their boyfriends' harem.

One afternoon, when they were both alone in the room, Rita was bold enough to challenge Bondawaa's manhood. "If you are a normal man, you cannot say that none of us here is attractive enough to kindle the manly fire in you," she said coquettishly, smiling and swaying her rumps. As she was doing this, her wrapper fell off, exposing her cute, appetizing contour. Her breasts were round and turgid, with their dark nipples pointing at Bondawaa. Her belly was flat; her hips curved beautifully, her legs slender and slightly hairy. She was now looking at him invitingly with her lips parted. He felt stormy between his thighs and lost control of himself. He held her by the wrist, his whole being trembling. She soon wrapped her stifling hand round him and planted an aggressive kiss on his lips.

They stood there trembling in each other's arms, with their hearts pounding. Her animal scent was very pleasant to the nostrils. Soon, a quick anger and realization overwhelmed Bondawaa. He held Rita's chin up and dealt her a sharp slap in the temple and gave her a cold smile. She recoiled from him and sat down, weeping quietly. He suddenly felt sorry for her. The encounter that day did not put Rita off at all. She continued to manifest her love to Bondawaa in several ways. He was in great trouble with her. But how can he make love to the fiancée of his close friend? One of the things Bondawaa cherished most in this world was his relationship with Keifa. He could not afford to make it break. His maternal grandmother had often warned him that three things sever human relationships in this world: money, woman, and the words that one utters! But avoiding Rita to maintain his friendship with Keifa was a difficult task.

Keifa's landlord grew fed-up with him and his cohort for overcrowding his compound. One day he called Bondawaa to his parlour and asked, "How many of you now live in that room?"

"Only two, sir, the rest are only here briefly" he lied. The landlord nodded his head in false acceptance. Their landlord was not the type of man to joke with. He was a party stalwart, a thug. He got the money with which he built the house through violence and banditry. He was one of those, Bondawaa was told, who had risked their lives and smeared their reputation to bring the ruling party into power and to keep it there. He was a very tough man. One would know it from the way he talked and walked.

Before he called Bondawaa to his parlour that day, their landlord had already done his research and known exactly what the truth was. He only wanted confirmation from him. But he was naive to have thought that Bondawaa would be straightforward with him in the circumstances. Some other landlords would have issued a written notice to evict them from the room, but their landlord used intimidation. He set his houseboy against them. The young man would treat Keifa and his team in the shabbiest manner; he would humiliate and harass them, and their landlord would not treat the matter seriously when reported to him. The houseboy became a real menace to them. Every plan to correct this ugly situation did not seem to work, being that the young man's master was such an influential man.

One morning, the houseboy deposited all the dirt he had swept from the staircase into a bucket containing the white briefs and vests of Keifa and Bondawaa soaked in water.

"Why have you done this?" Bondawaa asked him furiously, shaking with rage.

"Get out of my sight, bastard!" he answered, laughing at Bondawaa scornfully.

The houseboy was bulkier than anyone of them. He had always depended on the fact that none in Keifa's group would feel comfortable to engage him in a fight. Bondawaa was too angry to consider the houseboy's bulk. He landed a heavy and surprise buffet on his right jaw, and like a mighty cotton tree, he crashed into the gutter. Bondawaa stood right over him, waiting for him to get up. As soon as he did another blow landed in his right ear, down he fell into the gutter again. This time Bondawaa did not stand and wait, he kicked him in the face and his nose started to bleed. He continued to rain blows on him when his master descended the stairs: "pao, pao!" he gave Bondawaa two hot slaps with his iron-like palm. He jumped off the houseboy. Some hot sugary liquid filled his mouth. He spat it out. It was blood. His head was spinning round. "Come with me upstairs, I will teach these bush boys a lesson," the landlord said and went upstairs with his houseboy.

In the evening of the same day, when Bondawaa was walking along Banana Street, a neighbour, an elderly woman, called him and said, "My young man, from now onwards you must be careful with your landlord. He can do anything to you, and of course what will come out of it? Your parents are poor, you will just suffer quietly."

The landlord gave Keifa and his crowd an ejectment notice to vacate his room at the end of the month.

CHAPTER SEVENTEEN

The Girl from Makaya Village

Bondawaa bought a newspaper on his way to school one day but as usual he decided not to read it until he had gone back home. He was stunned by the headline, "The Minister of Information and Broadcasting Allegedly Involved in Ritual Murder." He put the paper aside and went across the street to buy few beers to drink while reading the insipid story about his friend, the only minister of government he had come close to and respected from that time onward. The newspaper article said that the minister had paid a hunter to kill a 10year-old girl at a village five miles away from Makaya. When they found the body, her vital parts had all been removed.

When Kathotha, the hunter, reported to the chiefs what he had found in the bush, he was advised to ignore the matter and not to go near the area any more until the matter died a natural death. He did not know how a matter such as that would die a natural death, and he was sure he would not sleep if the matter was not investigated, and the culprit brought to justice. He therefore ran to the police and reported the murder; little realizing that he would be the Second Accused in the child's murder case, with the Honourable Minister of Information and Broadcasting as the First Accused.

"The Honourable Minister of Information and Broadcasting, Maguey Tatame Thomas, is the most power-hungry nincompoop the country has ever created in its entire political history. He is not ready to stop at anything in his quest to climb to the highest position in the land, irrespective of the fact that the top is already filled, and capably and irrevocably filled," the article read.

"He is now pursuing his political ambition in the maximum-security ward of the state prison with the poor hunter setting traps for rats in the vicinity of that ward. The murder case against the two socially incompatible friends would be heard in the High Court in two weeks' time," the article continued.

Bondawaa put the newspaper down after reading the article, rose from the chair, walked out of the room, closed the door behind him and went for a walk. He took a long walk; he went well beyond the city centre and continued to go aimlessly when suddenly it dawned on him that the night was moving close to curfew time. If he were to walk back home now curfew would catch up with him. He searched his pocket for money to pay his way back but there was nothing there, and he began to run. He had run only a few hundred yards when he bumped into Keifa.

"Who is chasing you?" he asked.

"Curfew, you can see that it's only twenty minutes away and we are this far from the house," Bondawaa said, showing Keifa the time from his watch.

"But why didn't you take a taxi home, I am waiting for one," Keifa said. Bondawaa put his hands into both of his trousers pockets and turned them inside out. While he was doing this Keifa had flagged a taxi, "Let's go poor boy before it is curfew time," he said drawing Bondawaa into the taxi by the hand. By the

107

time they got home Bondawaa had resolved to visit the minister in prison, and to witness the court sittings.

CHAPTER EIGHTEEN

On the Move

Keifa moved his group from No. 1 Banana Street to No. 99 Winfred Lane. Getting this place required an enactment of a dramatic scenario. Landlord-tenant relation was one of the vexed issues in Gracetown at that time. Often it was under the dictates of the landlords that the tenants lived, particularly in a situation where the tenants and the landlords lived in the same premises or compound. But as the adage goes, the anthill that does not want human tread should not grow edible mushrooms. Keifa and his group urgently needed an apartment. With an ejectment notice on their back, their major concern was a place to rent. The facilities and conditions were secondary matters. The best method used in locating a vacant apartment in Gracetown then was to move along the streets at night looking at the houses. If one saw an apartment without light and window curtains, it was very likely that that apartment was vacant.

Moving along Winfred Lane one night, Keifa and Bondawaa saw an apartment without light and window curtains. It was the ground floor of a one-storey building. They walked up to a teenager they saw standing at the gate leading into the backyard of the house.

"Excuse me please, do you live here?" Keifa asked the teenager.

109

"Yes, this is my father's compound," he answered proudly.

"Could you please give us some information about the ground floor; I see that it is empty? We are desperately in need of a place to rent," Keifa said.

"The place is vacant quite all right, but who wants it?" the teenager asked.

"We," Keifa answered. The teenager smiled scornfully.

"I am very sorry, you can't get the apartment," he said still smiling.

"Why?" Keifa asked, almost breathless.

"Because my dad does not rent it to young and seemingly irresponsible people like you, sorry about my language." Man must live by his wits; Bondawaa thought very quickly and said to their young friend.

"Sorry dear, we want the place not for ourselves. Our uncle who is partially responsible for both of us has sent us on this errand."

"Where does your uncle work?"

"He is the Deputy Governor II of the Bank of Simbeck who has been transferred here from the Eastern Regional Office," Keifa lied.

"Oh, you should have thrown in those details earlier. What if I had just said no without giving reason? Please let us go upstairs and meet my dad," he led the way.

They met Mr. Fannah reclined in a settee. He was a pleasant looking man, fair complexioned, lean, and tall. His wife had just returned from the Hajj and was wearing a veil. Al-Haja Maimitu Fannah, as she was popularly referred to, was a tall, slender woman with

110

a gap in the middle of her upper teeth. Like most Al-Hajas in Gracetown, she had a gold tooth. She smiled most of the time, a strategy to exhibit the gold tooth and the fine gap in the middle of her upper teeth. Even at that first meeting, she looked overbearing and the ruler of the home. Both spouses did not have formal education, but their parlour exhibited an exquisite array of paintings and sculptures. There was a painting of Bai Bureh hanging on the wall, and many other heroes and ordinary people. The most striking of these paintings was that of a man collecting palm wine. He was depicted as having reached the crown of the palm tree, removed the gourd containing the wine and emptying the content into another gourd. The palm tree was very tall, yet the tapper was able to maintain his balance with maximum ease. Two men sat at the base of the palm tree waiting hungrily for the gourd to be lowered. The artist captured the scene so expertly that one could sense the string of expectation connecting the men at the base to the one up in the tree.

There was also a lavish display of sculptures as well. Bundo devil, Kongɔli, Matɔma, Gɔbɔi and other mask devils were placed in strategic places in the parlour. Bondawaa was so carried away by this superfluous display of artifacts that he started moving around the parlour slowly as if he was at an arts exhibition. As he moved around the parlour, Bondawaa kept on wondering how the love for one's culture could compromise his religious tenets.

"Yes, what do your friends want?" Mr. Fannah asked his son.

111

"These men are in search of a place to rent. They have just seen the apartment on the ground floor and want to talk to you about it."

Mr. Fannah gave Keifa and Bondawaa an enquiring look. A look pregnant with many questions: where are these young men from? What are their backgrounds? Are they responsible people? Won't they create problems for me if I accommodate them in my house? Keifa did not allow him to verbalize his thoughts before he responded. "We are looking for an apartment for our uncle, sir. He is the Deputy Governor II of the Bank of Simbeck on transfer from the Eastern Regional Office. We are his nephews, and we too are gainfully employed," he lied. Mr. Fannah asked them to come with their uncle to see him at the earliest possible time, since empty apartments were going like hot cakes. As they went down the steps, Bondawaa began to rack his brain about the drama that lay ahead of them. They needed an uncle, or at least somebody to pose as one. The plotting and acting of this drama needed an experienced dramatist and actors and actresses. The show had to go down well with their audience or else they would miss the apartment, and they could not afford to miss it.

Bondawaa had not stayed long in Gracetown before he started grappling with such a colossal accommodation problem. Back at Ngawobu if anybody had told him that somebody would shout at him or give him hot slaps for allegedly being an irresponsible tenant, he would have dismissed him as a senseless joker.

One Sunday evening, just two days after they had met Mr. Fannah about his house, Keifa and Bondawaa brought their uncle to see him. It was one of their friends who was financially stronger than all of them and was going to occupy one of the rooms in the apartment, that masqueraded as their uncle. He adorned himself in a large floating gown, which Bondawaa held at the hem from time to time to stop it from gathering dirt. Keifa carried their uncle's portfolio as well as his walking stick. The uncle had a voluminous cigar stuck to his mouth, but it was not lit, as he was not sure of the Fannah's stance on smoking. The Fannah family started to smell Keifa and his group well before they got to their parlour. The aroma of the perfume that they had bathed in was their forerunner. There was enough evidence from their appearance and manners that they were not only responsible, but that their uncle was also one of those diverting state funds to their private accounts overseas. "But why does he not have a mansion? Is he lavishing his wealth on women, or is he one of the few discrete ones?" Mr. Fannah's mind started to wander.

*****

When Keifa and his team settled in No. 99 they threw a house-warming party which was extremely extravagant. They contracted a nearby restaurant to cater for the occasion. It was a party for twenty, comprising only their intimate friends and some younger members of the Fannah family.

When the party had progressed for some time, they asked the most educated amongst them, a sixth former, Teddy Magoi, to give the welcome speech and purpose of the party. Their parlour was large enough to seat them and all their guests conveniently. It was a crazy and luxurious party.

"Ladies and we the men…emm-mm, I am very sorry, emm-mm, the city and western education has not got the better of me yet… no, not at all! Gentlemen and ladies for that matter…" he emptied the glass of beer he held in his hand, looked at each attendee in the face, smiled broadly and resumed. "I want to welcome you all to this very modest party. I hope you will agree with me that it is very modest. Our people say that the ant takes into its hole only what it can carry."

"True, true!" the others applauded.

"This party is modest because we are conducting it here in our common parlour, not at Cape Castle, the country's No. 1 restaurant."

"The plain truth, sir, you are saying nothing but the plain truth!" There was another round of applause.

"It is a modest party considering the number of invited guests. Only twenty; we cannot afford to invite more than that. It is modest because it has dug holes in our pockets, which will take months to fill. It is modest because it is going to dress us in a robe meant for the cream of society." The place became quiet, and everybody sobered up. Teddy was teasing himself and the rest of his team, they thought. His choice of the word modest was now becoming monotonous and unclear to everyone.

"But gentlemen and ladies, our people say that it is the paddle that you find in the boat that you use to row it. In the city you must throw your weight around for you to be accepted in certain social circles. That is what we are doing today, and that is exactly what we have called you here to help us do." One of the members of the Fannah family was now looking at Keifa in disbelief. Bondawaa became very uncomfortable, and so was Keifa.

"Now let me take this opportunity to welcome you all to this house-warming party. Please let us all fill our glasses, rise and drink to the health of all the occupants of this wonderful apartment, and the owners of the house." There was uproar. Soon the music was playing loudly, and most of the invitees were on their feet dancing. On instinct, Bondawaa turned around and there he saw Mr. Fannah peeping through one of the windows. As he rose to go and meet him, the man hurriedly climbed the stairs to their own apartment.

CHAPTER NINETEEN

No 99 Winfred Lane

Their apartment at No. 99 Winfred Lane was a modern convenience with three bedrooms, the largest of which had a built-in toilet. Five of them lived in this apartment. The master-room was occupied by their mock uncle, the second by Tamba, co-worker of Keifa and the third by Keifa, Teddy and Bondawaa. Their mock uncle was the Chief Bartender at the most prestigious hotel in Gracetown. Each day he returned from work, a good sum of money, some expensive cigarettes and a reasonable quantity of hard liquor accompanied him to the apartment. Under his auspices all the inmates lived like lords.

They had two servants to attend to their wants and needs, including taking care of the apartment. They were two obedient and hard-working young men. In the morning they would sweep and dust the rooms, clean the toilets and prepare breakfast. They would launder the clothes every four days. In the morning, before going to work, an occupant only needed to look in the general wardrobe for some clean outfit to wear. Their lunch and dinner were prepared by the numerous fiancées and girlfriends that they had. Collisions between members of these two groups were some of the many dramas that one enjoyed at No. 99.

Saturday and Sunday were special days of the week at No. 99. They referred to Saturday night as Cowboys Night and Sunday as the Holy Day. Their

116

Saturday would start at 9am with breakfast, followed by two hours of chat on any topic under the sun. This would be followed by a longish period of boozing, interspersed with light lunch and long and short worship sessions by pairs of worshippers. This would take them up to about 6:00 pm when they would all retire to their bedrooms for nothing less than four hours, to pick up energy to resume the evening session.

The evening session would take them to almost all the nightclubs in Gracetown. They had their own private car in which they made these trips. It was a taxi owned by their mock uncle. They would always start with the less important nightclubs and end with the more sophisticated. They would spend at most twenty minutes in each bar or restaurant. Everywhere they went they would replenish their beers, play the jackpot, dance, and then depart. Their last port of call would be where they would spend most of the night.

Sometimes they went in pairs. Bondawaa never really went in pair at any given time. He was always the odd man in the group, and there were all indications that his oddness was an embarrassment to his friends, and that they were planning to do something about it. Most of the time, their Holy Days were spent on the altar with the opposite sex, praying to Cupid. It was done in rotation. The female sex came in turns to receive what they called Holy Water. One Holy Day, an early worshipper came to the altar in room two. She arrived at 7:00 am to be precise. She had armed herself well enough to stimulate the love of her god. No sooner had she stepped into the parlour after Bondawaa had opened the door, than the aroma

117

of perfume permeated the whole apartment. She was tall, dark with thick long hair that flowed down to her shoulders. Her lips were thin and red. When she smiled, she displayed a perfect set of teeth, set on firm black gum. The look of this worshipper took Bondawaa's breath away. He stood looking at her, dumbfounded. "What a wonder of God's creation," he said to himself.

"I want to talk to Tamba, please," she said.

"Please come and sit down while I look for him," Bondawaa instructed, pointing to the settee. She sank into the seat stylistically, making sure that her skirt would not rumple. He turned the bolt and to his surprise the door opened. Tamba raised his head from the bed, roused by the creaking of the door, and he frowned.

"An angel is waiting in the parlour to worship with you," Bondawaa said light-heartedly.

"Please Bondawaa, don't spoil my Holy Day. I have made no bookings from early worshippers," he said, stretching his limbs and yawning.

"Look, the master room is empty. I will ask her to try altar one," Bondawaa said teasingly.

Tamba struggled out of the bed, wrapped himself in his cover cloth and walked to the door, limping. When he set eyes on the girl in the settee, his reaction was indescribable. "Come in, darling," he called, now mesmerized by the girl's beauty. Soon, reggae hymns were filtering in from room two, drowning the several voices that usually greeted the rising sun. It was a sunny day; the beam from the morning sun already illuminated the parlour. Intermittently, there were echoes of halleluiah, amen, ha-ha-ha-le-lu-u-u-ja-ah, a-a-aa-aa-m-e-n, as the pair of worshippers were being filled with the Holy Spirit.

Teddy joined Bondawaa in the parlour, looking anxious. He had never seen Teddy in that condition before. He had always looked spirited, very playful, and full of humour.

"Do you have a complaint about Martha?" Bondawaa asked.

"Forget about that woman, I can always put her under control. It is something else that is worrying me. It concerns my whole future."

"Can we talk about it?"

"Sure, Bondawaa, that is why I have joined you," Teddy said, shifting back and forth in the chair.

"Yes, please."

"It is about my schooling. I am having a hell of a problem with it. You know how far away we live from school; with the current transportation problem I get to school late every day. Coupled with that is the problem of accommodation. There is no convenient place at home here for me to sit down and compile my notes, do my assignments and study. I want to apply for admission in college next year, but I want to pick up a pupil teaching job from now to that time; how about that?" he sounded Bondawaa's opinion.

"If I were you, I would continue until the end of this academic year."

"But Bondawaa, what will I benefit by continuing? Nothing! Seven or so months of teaching will earn me

119

some money to buy some of the basic things I would need in college."

"You are the one wearing the shoes, Teddy; you know exactly where they hurt you."

Tamba had just appeared in the parlour walking together with his co-worshipper, both smiling at Teddy and Bondawaa gaily when a tallish, hefty girl pushed the main door and walked into the parlour. She walked up strait to Tamba and embraced him.

"Say boy, I've caught up with you today! You are hardly found in this place. From now until dusk we are going to be together," the new worshipper said, still holding Tamba in her arms. Tamba became pale and transfixed, searching his mind for something to tell his buoyant new arrival. He was a chicken-hearted, lean fellow not experienced in handling a problem such as this. He was trembling physically.

"But I have no appointment with you. Why do you have to spend the day with me?" He asked.

"Come on darling, you want to refuse me now? What has suddenly gone into your stupid head?" She asked, now dragging Tamba towards the room. Tamba was struggling weakly, unable to put up a strong resistance. He looked at Teddy and Bondawaa, his eyes imploring them to help. The first worshipper stood with her eyes moist. She was the aristocratic type, one who would not put up a fight in such a situation. She would prefer to cry quietly until her grief goes away.

As Tamba was being dragged to the entrance of his room, the aristo girl could no longer control her emotions. She found herself pleading in tears, "Please rescue my darling from this monster; he does not love her. Please help!" She did not know that she was the so-called monster's actual target. She was only being provoked to talk. Before Tamba and Bondawaa could intervene, her dress had been torn off her slender body and was receiving hot slaps. It was a grotesque show with the aristo girl trying to cover her body, least minding the blows that were developing blisters in her mouth. Teddy and Bondawaa quickly drew the curtain across the ugly scene. It would be inimical for them if a member of the Fannah family, their landlords, should watch the show.

Teddy had taken up employment as a pupil teacher in a primary school close to Bondawaa's, also in the afternoon shift. By 11:45 am every Monday through to Friday, they would leave the house together for school and would return home latest 6:30 pm.

Teddy and Bondawaa discovered that the lifestyle at No. 99 was not good for both as they had ambitions to further their education. They discovered that it was not good for them to be drunk most of the time when they had to prepare their lesson notes and to read novels, at least two per month, to improve their English. They also discovered that life at No. 99 was forcing them to live above their means. They used all kinds of methods to stay aloof from the rest of the group, but it was impossible.

Coming home in the evening after school, they often found someone boozing who would call them to join him. "Hey teachers, there is some beer here to drink, plenty of it. Why not join me? Life is meant to be lived, and to be lived well, so that you won't regret it if you should die today or tomorrow," the person would say. So, the invincible hands of licentiousness engulfed them firmly at No.99.

One Friday evening at about ten o'clock, Uncle came home from work with a young girl; she was irresistibly beautiful, though life seemed to have been cruel to her for the past several years. She was about five feet nine inches, slender and dark with prominent tribal marks on both cheeks.

As they entered his room, Uncle called Bondawaa in. No sooner did he enter than Uncle said, "Bondawaa, this is Tonya; she says she knows you and has been longing to meet and talk with you. The two of you can talk in here until tomorrow morning. No need to hurry at all," he said as he left, locking them in.

"Excuse me, do I know you?" Bondawaa asked the girl, feeling uncomfortably embarrassed.

"We will know each other very well tonight, Bondawaa. Don't worry," she answered, eyeing him hungrily. When they had first entered the parlour, she looked placid and innocent, as it were, led like a sheep to a slaughterhouse. But she was soon giddy and coquettish. She lay in the bed and began to roll back and forth, giggling like a child who has just been given a new toy.

"Do you have any idea why he has behaved to us like this, Tonya?" he asked his voice hoarse. She got up from the bed and held Bondawaa by the hand and said, "Please don't worry my baby, I love you very dearly and I am going to keep you extremely happy and comfortable tonight." She planted a kiss on his right cheek. It was warm. He recoiled confusedly, rushed to the door, and shook the bolt, but it was locked. He sighed and faced the girl again.

"Jesus, I cannot understand this stupid act. How can Uncle lock me up in a room alone with a girl I've never met before," he exploded.

"You are simply refusing to understand, but as a grown up you should know by now why. Your friends are afraid that you are not virile and have asked me to come and perform some ceremonies for you," she said with an animated laugh.

"But that is not their business. They have merely brought you here to waste your time. They cannot force me to..."

"You are in for blackmail, so you have to comply," she interrupted.

"What do you mean?"

"They say you are not a man, no matter what claims you make about your manhood. I am here to prove them right or wrong. They are all waiting for my report. You must prove to me that you are a man, Bondawaa, if you certainly are. I am paid to tell them the truth," she said and sat up in the bed, quite relaxed now.

"I cannot understand this senseless idea at all," he said, pacing the massive room, with Tonya now looking at him sympathetically.

"Please come and sit by me, you don't have to work yourself up like that over such a petty matter. You are attractive; I just don't know what is wrong with you." As he sat down, she caressed him gently and her fingers began to explore his body expertly."

"But Tonya, why did you allow yourself to be used like this?" He asked, beginning to get interested in her.

"Money, Bondawaa, money. In Simbeck today, a good number of us can do anything for money. But it is not our fault, we must survive," she said, looking away from him. To his surprise, she was weeping softly, her fingers resting numbly on his body. As her tears rolled, he was suddenly overwhelmed by sympathy for this sheer stranger to the extent that he held her in his arms and kissed her tenderly. She clung to him helplessly and wept freely. He wiped her face, and soon the Holy Spirit possessed them. There were murmurs of hallelujah, amen. When the Holy Spirit departed from them, they lay quietly, looking at the ceiling.

"Why did you cry, Tonya?" He broke the silence. She was soon crying all over again, the tears running down her cheeks unchecked.

"I have gone through a series of bitter experiences in life, Bondawaa – even at this early age. It is not my intention to be on the street having carnal relationship with every male that can pay me for doing so. It is a painful and dehumanizing business. I do not cherish it at all, but I cannot do otherwise." She had now stopped crying and was wiping her face with the back of her hand.

"How did it all begin?" he asked.

"It is a long story, but I will try to be very brief," she said, looking away from him.

"My plight started when I got pregnant in form three. My parents drove me from home to join the one who had impregnated me. He did his best to make me happy but apparently, he was ill prepared for the task. He and I lived in a very tiny cellar, and our food was always grossly inadequate.

Aside from all this, we grew to love and respect each other, and had an ardent desire to survive."

She turned to him suddenly and was now looking directly in his face. "A couple of months later, our baby came; I was only fifteen years old. It was a healthy baby boy, an effigy of his father. We loved and cherished him. The rains were heavy that year and food was difficult to come by. Our tiny room was always damp. The poor boy contracted pneumonia and died. I became very aggrieved and wept for two days without eating. My only desire then was to die, but my darling assured me that we could have another one soon and that it would live." She wrapped her hands around Bondawaa and was weeping quietly again.

"You have been a brave girl all along. You don't need to break down now," he said stroking her thick hair. She rose from the bed and began to pace the room thoughtfully.

"After the baby's death, my darling left me to go in search of fortune in the diamond mine. Two months passed without a word from him, three months, four; and I started going out at night to look for money to feed myself. After one year it became a trade for me. Through this shameless trade, I'm able to feed and clothe myself. But it is a real hard life, Bondawaa. We are misused and abused each night we go out." She came back to the bed, opened her handbag, took out a mirror and some cosmetics, re-did her make-up and was ready to go.

"Sorry that your friends connived with me to corrupt your life. Hope you will forgive me." She went to the door and knocked at it three times. The message got home, the key turned in the lock and the door was flung open. The girl walked gingerly into the parlour, and there was applause.

When Bondawaa went to bed that night, many images invaded his mind: images of numerous unwanted babies thrown into dustbins and gutters; images of street boys idling in parks, cinema halls and other entertainment centres; images of disabled people sitting in strategic places in Gracetown begging alms; images of prison centres full of young people immured for different shades of crimes; images of young men and women parading the streets of Gracetown frustrated to insanity; images of poverty amidst affluence; images of a huge number of university graduates going in search of employments that do not exist; images of the health, educational and other vital systems at the verge of collapse; an image of a society where corruption has been institutionalized; an image of Tonya carrying a dead baby in her arms. He began to weep for her.

CHAPTER TWENTY

Bondawaa's Troubles

Bondawaa has been making persistent efforts to visit the incarcerated former Minister of Information and Broadcasting. When he finally got an appointment to meet him, Bondawaa did not sleep. "What will I tell Mr. Thomas tomorrow when I meet him, as he is in such a trouble?" Bondawaa kept on asking himself the same question again and again. At 2:00 am he rose from the bed and started to scribble down something. "First I will introduce myself and bring to his attention where we met for the first time," he wrote down. "But his mind is so clouded now, and we have met only once. Chances are that he may even think I have been sent there by his enemies to pick words from his mouth. Worse still, I have never visited a prisoner before. I do not know the limitations they put on people who go to visit him." Bondawaa continued to scribble down. "But I have to meet him and tell him that I admire him and ask him to be courageous and have faith in his God in the face of all that lies ahead of him, and I will salute him and then prostrate to him before I walk out," he resolved.

Bondawaa put the notes under his pillow and soon fell asleep. It was now 5:30 am. A crowd has gathered in front of the Central Prisons and Bondawaa rushed there to find out what was going on.

. "Are they freeing some prisoners?" He asked breathless as he ran to the place.

127

"No, they are displaying the head of Mr. Thomas. He faced the gallows five o'clock this morning. It is sad, but that is the Simbeck we live in. Watch your steps always, young man," the middle-aged man told him.

"No, they have no right to kill him. They are calling for a revolution; the youth will rise against them. This is their idol, no one has right to kill him without the due process of the law." He yelled as he ran.

"Don't be foolish young man, and do not joke with the authorities. As you can see, the NPDs have littered the entire city. They have been instruction to shoot anyone who makes trouble over the hanging of the former Minister of Information and Broadcasting," the man yelled after Bondawaa. He woke up from the sleep, sweating and shaking.

*****

A woman in love is more dangerous than a snake that has been scotched. Rita was a snake Bondawaa had scotched. On many occasions he had seen her struggling for an opportunity to catch him in her trap. She looked for an opportunity in the bathroom, in the toilet, in the kitchen, in the bedroom, on the beach, everywhere.

When Bondawaa and Keifa got No. 99 Winfred Lane for themselves, they rented a place for Rita and Martha at No. 16 Biala Street. Keifa and Teddy spent more time at No. 16 than No. 99.

One day Bondawaa was alone at No. 99 after everybody had gone to work. He was convalescing after a severe attack of malaria. He was just about falling asleep after having read a crime novel for about two hours, when he heard someone knocking at the front door. When he opened it, he saw Rita standing in front of him, holding a basket. She soon flooded him with smiles, the type that always jarred on him with uncanny unpleasantness. With Rita in the parlour his ailment heightened. His heartbeat became rapid, his blood pressure went up, and his head began to spin.

Standing before this Eve, Bondawaa did not know exactly what to do, whether to shout her out or to allow the two of them alone in the house. The vast vacant house then became silent. Soon, it began to echo the throbbing of his heart. "It does not harm to be polite," Bondawaa recalled his mother's popular maxim and smiled back at Rita. His was a dry smile, sapped by confusion and torment.

Bondawaa's mother was a model of the traditional African woman who believed in doing good things all the time, even if she was getting evil in return. She was placid, obedient, and believed that there was no need to rush for the good things in life. "Obey and respect those who are older and in authority over you, your turn will then come one fine day," she would always admonish Bondawaa when he was returning to work from leave. While he blessed his mother for her pieces of advice, he sometimes felt that she influenced his life in a rather negative way. A man should not be too submissive and easy going.

"Why are you here, Rita?" he asked sullenly.

"Because you are sick and in this big house alone with nobody to give you love. Let us go into the room, I have some pepper soup here for you." His head stopped swimming. The voices of the pepper birds singing in the tree by the house started to pervade the parlour. He also began to hear very clearly the ticking of the wall clock. While in the room Rita forced Bondawaa to lie down and prop up his head on the pillow so that she could feed him with a spoon. Some kind of helplessness dawned on him as he saw himself being fed like a baby. As he was drinking the soup, she caressed him tenderly.

"Love is more potent than medicine and food, Bondawaa, particularly love coming genuinely from deep down a woman's heart."

"I have always defined and redefined your love and it has meant to me, without the slightest shift, a ploy intended to sever my relationship with Keifa." Rita became pale, and her fingers went numb on the spoon. Soon she was sobbing softly and murmuring something to herself. She splashed the remaining soup in Bondawaa's face and ran out saying, "Proud and worthless fool, I'll teach you a lesson."

As Bondawaa lay in the bed, blinded by the pepper soup, he began to think of Matu. Her benefactor, the pregnant man, had been sent on transfer to one of the provincial headquarters as an Administrative Head, and had asked her to go with him. When Matu was around Bondawaa did not only get material support from her, but he also had a place to hide himself to evade naked seduction from the fiancée of his intimate friend and brother, Keifa. "What has arrogance got to do with this, when I am merely trying to stop you from messing up my brotherly relationship with my friend?" he murmured to himself as he came down the bed to clean the mess Rita had made. He changed the bed linens, swept the room, opened the windows for fresh air to come in, and then went to the bathroom to bathe and change.

At the beginning of each month Keifa, Teddy and Bondawaa would contribute some money, which their ladies, Rita, and Martha, would use to cook for all of them until the end of that month. Two days following the soup incident, Rita wrote to tell Bondawaa there was no more money left for cooking and it was only the fifteenth day of the month. What hurt him more was the tone of the letter. It was harsh, and accused Bondawaa of things he was not guilty of. He wrote her a mocking reply. Her reaction was to starve him for the rest of the month. Keifa's response to the misunderstanding between Rita and Bondawaa was not to be on speaking terms with him. He felt betrayed by his best friend.

Keifa and Bondawaa became close friends when the former was in form three, and the latter in form two. They had inexplicable admiration and kindly feelings for each other. At Ngawobu High they did most things in common; they were like siblings. When they came to Gracetown, their intention was to work concertedly towards achieving their goals in life. They got on well together until the rift between Rita and Bondawaa. Their secret dream was to use formal education as the key to socio-economic mobility for themselves and the younger members of their family. Their strategy was to put their resources together and send one of them to the United States of America, and for the forerunner to in turn create an opportunity for the other to join him. Unwittingly, however, the funds were not saved in the same account with an instruction for dual signatory before withdrawal.

They worked fervently towards this noble goal for months; each one of them was saving a big share of his earnings every month. But apparently, this dream stood miles and miles away from them.

There came a time when it appeared like a fantasy. They each had their restraints. Keifa was a swanky person and lover of women. As his account grew, he pinched from it to buy a new jacket suit or the latest model of shoes. He pinched from it to take a date to an expensive nightclub, and they would both return home drunk. On the other hand, Bondawaa would withdraw a whole month's salary to pay a brother's school fees and other charges or to send back home a relative who would come to him unexpectedly with his or her problems. He would receive from home a message about hunger and would be obliged to send there a bag of rice or the better part of his salary. In this way their savings refused to grow.

"You have your cousins in the States, why can't you write and ask them for help?" Bondawaa asked Keifa one day. Keifa's countenance changed completely when he was asked that question.

"Yes, but we did not like one another when they left this country. And since they left some ten years or so ago, none has ever written to me," Keifa explained.

"You are poor, and you say you don't eat dog meat?" Bondawaa teased Keifa. Eventually, he was able to convince him to write and ask one of his cousins in the United States to pave his way to join him there.

After four months of waiting, and Keifa and Bondawaa had begun thinking that it was probably not worth writing for help, a biggish envelope was delivered to Bondawaa for Keifa Seppeh-Bengeh by a postman. It came from Ohio. Bondawaa wanted to know its content very badly, but he had to wait for Keifa to return from work. Keifa came back home that evening exhausted; consequently, Bondawaa waited until he bathed and ate before he gave him the letter. They opened it eagerly. It contained application forms from Ohio University in Athens. They embraced, for clearly, that was a giant stride towards their goal.

Following the exchange of the sour letters between Rita and Bondawaa, days grew into weeks, weeks into months and still Keifa did not talk to Bondawaa; and he was now responsible for his own feeding. He became inconceivably misplaced by this development, particularly for the fifteen days to the end of the month that Rita stopped dishing food for him. Some evenings, he fed on roasted cassava and occasionally ate at cookery houses.

Eating at third-rate cookery houses was not a pleasant practice for Bondawaa. Before he came to Gracetown he had been told a multiplicity of stories about the malpractices of those who run such houses, all in the bid to make massive profits. Some were said to cook dog meat, others monkeys and vultures. Some

133

others were said to worship devils to attract more customers.

With all these biases in his mind for local eating-houses, it was an ordeal for Bondawaa to eat there at the beginning. In addition to these stories, there were a lot of other irregularities about some of these places. The dishes and cups were not properly washed; the places reeked of stale food and all kinds of people ate there, some with putrid sores, and others with contagious diseases.

Bondawaa kept on changing cookery houses. He was not primarily looking for good quality food. He simply did not want to be associated with one. In fact, he went to an eating-house only when it was dark. He did not want any of his pupils, or well-placed fellow teachers to find him there. However, he grew to favour a particular eating-house because it was hygienic. He ate there three times a week and distributed the remaining four days among other eating-houses.

One day when Bondawaa was eating at his favourite place, two teenage girls quietly went to him and asked, "Are you Mr. Ndoma? We are very pleased to meet you."

"What an obscure place for such cute girls to meet me for the first time, and who must have told them about me?" he wondered. His mouth remained crammed with the food; a mixture of rice and cassava leaves sauce, as the girls stood gazing at him. Bondawaa managed to swallow the stuff. He left the rest of the food, quite to his dissatisfaction, and walked out with what he regarded as devilish angels.

"My name is Josephine," one said.

"I am Omotunde, you teach our sister in school," the other said. Bondawaa felt embarrassed and stood transfixed, playing with the watch on his wrist.

"I have been betrayed," he said to himself. Josephine, Omotunde and Bondawaa had a brief conversation in which they told him the name of their sister he taught, their address, and invited him to visit them at home.

When Bondawaa arrived at the home of the Cokersons at No. 44 Batson Street on a Sunday afternoon, the whole family, a relatively small one, was at home to receive him. He was met at the door by Josephine, Omotunde and Christiana, their sister who was Bondawaa's pupil. The house, an archaic looking structure, constructed probably during the time of the early Re-captives, did not appeal to him from the outside. When he was led in, however, it was a completely different scenario. It was opulently furnished. The carpet was fluffy. There was a television set in the right-hand corner, and a piano in the left-hand corner of the massive parlour. The window curtains were ingeniously selected to match the wall paint and the carpet. It was, beyond all doubts, a beautiful set-up.

Bondawaa sank into an armchair that was facing Mr. and Mrs. Cokerson. They were a couple in their early forties, with five children: Josephine, Omotunde, Christiana and two boys. "I am happy to introduce my teacher, Mr. Bondawaa Ndoma, to my father Mr. Ayo Cokerson, my mother Mrs. Nancy Cokerson, my sisters Josephine and Omotunde Cokerson, and my brothers Robert and Francis Cokerson. Of course, Mr.

135

Ndoma knows my name very well," Christiana completed the introduction. There was giggling from the younger members of the family, but Mr. Cokerson encouraged Christiana not to mind them.

"None of them could have performed as marvelously as you did. Not even those in secondary school," Mr. Cokerson said, smiling a smile of assurance at his daughter.

Three of the children were in primary school: Christiana, Robert, and Francis. As Bondawaa had lunch with them that afternoon, he was asked by Mrs. Cokerson to consider the possibility of conducting private classes for their primary school children. This was arranged, and he had to meet them at their home for lessons three times a week. The fee was encouraging. Bondawaa went to college two years later, and the Cokersons continued to be his family friends even after college.

CHAPTER TWENTY-ONE

Keifa and Bondawaa

The silence between Keifa and Bondawaa protracted unduly, and every now and then Bondawaa was suffering from the want of homemade food and the loss of a fond, intimate and genuine friendship – the friendship which was the magnet that attracted him to Gracetown, and the pliers that held him there firmly. Now that it had let off its hold of Bondawaa, he was drifting in every sense of the word.

Bondawaa prepared his lessons well at home, but when it came to delivering them to the pupils, he found himself fumbling. He became sulkier by the week. Their Head Teacher, a keen observer and friend of her teachers, called Bondawaa into her office one day and said, "Mr. Ndoma, I have observed a marked change in you these days. You look rather crestfallen and not giving your best, may I share your worries with you, please?" Bondawaa started wondering whether he should tell this woman that he was dispirited because his best friend was not talking to him any longer; a Gracetonian, one born and bred in the city, a woman who he thought did not understand the intricacies of rural life, life based on communalism.

"It is one of those challenges that young men face, particularly when they are far away from their homes. I will try to get over it soon. But if I don't, I will certainly seek your help," Bondawaa told the Head Teacher evasively.

137

The month was April, Bondawaa and many other people were bathing in the sea at Number Three River. Despite the lack of proper care of her beaches, Simbeck has one of the most beautiful beaches in the world. The sand grains were even, smooth, amber, and warm, having been beaten the whole day by the scorching dry season sun. The music of the birds was drowned by the voices of people engaged in diverse activities here and there. It was one of those Easter outings. The beach was flooded with all shades of people. It was very difficult for one to move from one point to the other because of the crowd.

Some people were drinking, others dancing to the conglomerate of music that drowned all other sounds, including the regular splashing of the sea on the shore. A host of others lay on their backs away from the bustling crowd, looking at the sun loitering on the afternoon sky.

Keifa and some swimmers had swum to the deep and were engulfed in the silvery foam of the sea. Bondawaa yearned for the foam, admiring the courage of Keifa and his friends as they withstood the turbulent coil of the sea, which generated the foam. Soon, Bondawaa found himself swimming towards them smiling; hoping Keifa would smile back at him, that he would get united with him in this current of silvery foam. He laughed as he swam, knowing fully well that even in River Tɛbɛlɛh back in Ngawobu, he, Bondawaa, was a better swimmer than Keifa. Bondawaa was laughing so much that he accumulated a lot of air in his lungs. He became puffy and started gasping for breath. He was already in the deep, a good distance away from the bank where all the sensualities were going on, but not yet in the foam. He lost most of his energy and began to sink. Each time he dived he swallowed a good quantity of water before he managed to come up again. There was no more time for laughter.

"I am dying, I have to save myself," he resolved. Each time Bondawaa submerged he made a bold move to come up again. The last granules of energy left in him were diminishing with every submersion he made. Everybody was now looking at him. Keifa was smiling at him, but he never made any rescue move.

"Is he banking on my fertile skills in swimming, he should come and save me, or I am finished. He will soon come and lead me out by the hand, and I'll embrace him on the bank. We will be united again, and this time never to be set apart by an Eve," Bondawaa kept on hoping. He went down with no more energy left in him to come up again. While going down, two strong hands held him by both arms, lifted him to the surface and started pushing him towards the bank.

Lying on the bank, helpless and blinded by the water that kept on slapping him in the face, Bondawaa held the hand of his rescuer firmly.

"Oh Keifa, I knew you would save my life. I knew our dispute would be put right by this near-drowning episode," he said gasping.

"Bondawaa, your rescuer is not Keifa. I don't know if there is an indelible difference between the two of you or not. He preferred asking me to save you to him doing it," Paliwaa explained. While lying on the bank in the hot sand throwing up gallons of water,

Bondawaa started to wonder what exactly Rita would have told Keifa to make him ignore him even when he was at the verge of drowning. He woke up from the dream shivering, and there was Keifa occupying the other side of the same bed snoring softly, his mouth slightly open.

Bondawaa wrote to tell Keifa that he would move out of No. 99 Winfred Lane in a month's time. It was a difficult decision to make, but a necessary one. It was most distressing to live in the same room and yet be enemies. Even as Bondawaa was going away, he was firmly resolved that whatever he might have suffered in the hands of Keifa, or how strongly they might have poisoned his mind for him, he would never be his enemy in this life or another to come.

He therefore decided to put a distance between them, which he thought would eventually heal their differences. As he wrote the letter, Bondawaa kept on asking himself why he should not simply discuss with Keifa what had led to the misunderstanding between Rita and him. But the possibility that Keifa would believe his own side of the story was, in his assessment of the whole situation, very slim. He therefore decided to keep this unpleasant scenario a secret.

Bondawaa's address after No. 99 Wilfred Lane was 444F Kongobay Road, a long and popular street in Gracetown. Without going to his place to see how suitable it was, Bondawaa arranged to live with one of his co-teachers, Mr. Kandi. Mr. Kandi started teaching with a Teachers Certificate just when Bondawaa passed for Class Three (Standard One); the very year

Simbeck had its independence. He was a Senior Teacher and one of the few who had the Teachers Certificate on the staff. Notwithstanding his long service in the teaching field, Mr. Kandi's success – social, economic and what have you – was eroded by his excessive love for alcohol.

When Bondawaa moved to his senior colleague's residence, he was totally disappointed. Mr. Kandi's apartment consisted of a room and a parlour that was crying bitterly for basic furniture. Sharing this apartment with him was one of the traumatic experiences Bondawaa went through in Gracetown. Mr. Kandi was most of the time drunk on locally distilled wine known as *ɔmɔle*. Any time salaries were paid he would drink excessively for one full week. When Bondawaa had his first experience of this, he bought a mat, which he spread on the floor in the parlour to sleep on every night; to avoid the smell of stale locally distilled wine.

It was exactly four months since Bondawaa broke company with Keifa. He was lying on the mat one Saturday morning, not in any hurry to get up, as he was not going to work that day, when somebody tapped on the door. He sprang up hurriedly, folded the mat, quickly put it under the bed in the room and then came back to the parlour and said: "Who is that this early morning? It is so ungodly a time you know."

"It is I Keifa. Please open the door." Bondawaa's heart sank. "What must have brought him here this early morning? Is somebody dead back at home, my

141

father dead?" His mind wandered and wandered in that brief spell.

"Please wait, I'm coming," Bondawaa said in a husky voice. He opened the door, and there was Keifa standing, his own Keifa, clean shaven, looking at Bondawaa straight in the eyes with his face covered with smiles, pure and affectionate smiles. He stood at the door transfixed, still looking at Bondawaa. He was quick to learn that Keifa had good tidings for him, and that that very Saturday morning they were going to re-unite.

"Come in, don't stand at the door. There are some chairs in here for us to sit," he said.

They both went into the parlour quietly. Soon, a long spell of silence was cast over them. They kept looking at each other and smiling. As they smiled rather endlessly, Bondawaa kept on thinking deep down his heart that Keifa was the right person to break the silence. "After all he has something to tell me. He will not come all the way here only for us to smile in each other's face."

Before they parted company at No. 99 Winfred Lane, Bondawaa and Keifa used to go on bus ride early on Saturday mornings. As rustics from the province, this was a novelty for them. They would prepare their breakfast and lunch packs late Friday evening in order that they would catch the first bus from Winfred Lane junction for Goodlight in the Western Rural district. Because of heavy traffic around the east end and the centre of Gracetown, it took them about two hours to get to Goodlight. They would have breakfast there, go to their favourite spot, have some beers, and set for the second leg of the excursion, which would take them to Yoke land. By the time they got there, it would be around 10:30 or 11:00 am, and they would go to the home of a palm wine tapper friend who usually rekindled in them the memories of home.

Their friend, Makio, would then take them to a clearing in the bush and bring kegs of palm wine for them, straight from the gourd, no adulteration. While his friends would be dinking leisurely, Makio would be busy entertaining them with indigenous songs, accompanied on the *Kondi* (a local musical instrument with four flat iron bars stretched over a hole bore in the middle of a flat can). When they become drunk, they would join Makio to sing and dance. They would dance and shout until they get exhausted and then go to sleep on beds made of plain logs and fronds. They would wake up very hungry, eat their lunch and then bathe in the sea for some time before they go back home via Waterland, no longer using the route they had used to come. They would have gone round the peninsula by the time they get back home.

They had stopped making such expeditions together for a long time now, Bondawaa thought as he waited for Keifa to break the silence.

"Bondawaa", his name echoed and re-echoed in the tiny parlour, "I'll be leaving for the United States of America in four days. Sorry that I'm telling you about it only now. I just returned from Ngawobu late yesterday evening. I was there to say goodbye to my parents, especially my grandmother, who may not be alive upon my return. My ticket, passport and visa are

143

ready," Keifa said as he handed Bondawaa the package. He looked at the contents for a brief while.

"May God bless you, Keifa, our dream has come true at long last," he said handing him back the package.

"Indeed, my brother, I'll send an air ticket for you to join me as soon as I get settled down in that country. You and I have struggled here together; and the idea to seek assistance from my cousins in the US originated from you. You should come and join me to work out what we can do together in that country of great opportunities." As Keifa was decanting his heart to Bondawaa, they were brought into each other's arms by a kind of magnetic force.

CHAPTER TWENTY-TWO

Mr. Thomas

An attractive, young female prison warden ushered Bondawaa in to see Mr. Thomas at the Simbeck Central Prison. It was on a bright Saturday morning. However, as he entered the precinct, an uncanny chill struck Bondawaa, and his lips began to quiver. "Please sit here and wait for Mr. Thomas; he will join you soon," the officer said and left Bondawaa in a waiting room with four wobbly chairs. Bondawaa's heart was beating a bit fast as he asked himself: "Will this man recognize me; will he even listen to me; am I not merely going to add to his agony this morning?" He began to rehearse in his mind the notes he had made for this occasion a couple of weeks ago. Every single word of those notes had come back fresh to his memory. He was now ready to meet his friend, the only politician he admires in the whole of Simbeck. He rose to his feet and began to pace the room thoughtfully. Soon, another door leading to the waiting room creaked and Mr. Thomas was led in, this time by a no-nonsense looking warden whose eyes were as red as a spitting cobra.

"You are Bondawaa?" he asked.

"Yes, sir."

"Bondawaa what?"

"Ndoma, sir."

"Mr. Ndoma, you have only twenty minutes to talk to your friend and be warned that every single wall here has ears." He said and departed.

As the stern looking warden departed, Mr. Thomas smiled broadly at Bondawaa and said, "My God, young man, you mean after our first meeting in my parlour in Makaya, you still remember me and have been following my calamity all along?" Bondawaa returned his smile and shook his hand warmly. They embraced and Bondawaa began to weep in the man's arm quietly. "Please don't do that, my young friend. Let us sit down, we have a lot to discuss, and we have only twenty minutes. We should not waste it on shedding tears." Mr Thomas had lost the charm that attracted Bondawaa to him at their first meeting, coupled with his humility and hospitality. His hair was unkempt, his beard not shaven since he was immured into the prison. He had lost weight considerably and was looking weak.

"I am Bondawaa. I am pleasantly surprised that you can still recall where we met for the first and only time. The event was that I went to your house in Makaya to look for my friend, who you told me was your younger brother."

"I remember you very well, not because I have a retentive memory, but that you are one of the few people who have gone through the rigours to come and find me in this dungeon. Now, most of my family members and good friends have abandoned me. It seems to me as if they are all gullible enough to accept the allegation my political enemies have made against me."

146

"I am here because I admire and respect you. Of all the politicians in Simbeck, you are the one and only one that has a human face. You are a victim of political animosity. I have come all the way to let you know this before anything should happen to you."

"If I should be hanged today, I will depart this world a happy man, and I will go and meet my God in peace. This is a message of exoneration. I am sure God has sent you to come and console me with this message. The courts are not going to tell me this. Even if they want to, they cannot. Those who run the courts have their jobs and lives to protect. I will not blame them."

"But when did the life of man become as precarious as that of a fowl's in Simbeck? You can take the life of a fowl today because you have a visitor and there is no other meat to cook for him."

"Right now, my life is less valuable than that of a fowl. When the fowl is slaughtered, the entire family including the visitor, feast on it. But when I am going to be hanged, my enemies will dump my remains in a grave in a cemetery reserved for common criminals."

"But no verdict has been passed on you yet."

"I am sure you have been following the court proceedings closely. It is only a matter of time; my only concern is that poor hunter who raised the alarm about the murder, like any other good citizen would have done. He should not be sacrificed together with me." Bondawaa started weeping again, and this time Mr. Thomas joined him. The stern prison officer walked in and led Mr. Thomas away.

147

*****

Three weeks after their meeting in the Simbeck Central Prison, Bondawaa was fast asleep when Mr. Thomas entered the room and sat by his side on the bed.

"It is my turn to visit you, my young friend, to bid you goodbye and make a confession, since I am going to be hanged early this morning," he said smiling wryly. Bondawaa jumped from the bed and put his hands on his head and said,

"Oh no, it cannot be this early."

"It is just five hours away now."

"You mean you paid the hunter to kill that innocent girl?" "That is not the confession I have come to make. I have no hands in her cruel murder."

"What then is your crime?"

"My crime is that of the snake charmer, who eventually gets bitten by the snake he dances with and dies. That is what is happening to me now. I was playing with a viper, thinking that it will never bite me." "What do you mean?"

"I have been part of a viper-infested political dance all this time, thinking the least that they were developing fangs for me."

"Please make yourself clearer."

"I mean I have shamelessly been part of all the political machinations that have been going on in Simbeck by the PAPP: vote rigging, unopposed elections, bad economic policies, suppression of opposing voices and opinions. I mean all the

148

malpractices that have brought this country to her knees."

"But that is not what you are being accused of?"

"Murder, they say, but I will not be the only victim of such a calculated political elimination ploy when I face the gallows early this morning."

"But, but…"

"I had ample chance to quit, take my entire family with me and live in exile, but I stayed put."

Bondawaa grabbed hold of Mr. Thomas firmly. "You are not going anywhere. Let them come and meet you here and I will tell them what I feel about them." They began to struggle, and Mr. Thomas overpowered Bondawaa and disappeared from the room. He opened the door to look for his friend, but there was no trace of him outside. To his surprise, a prison truck ran across with neck-breaking speed led by a pick-up van full of the National Protective Division officers, all of them armed to the teeth. This same truck was accompanied by two pick-up vans loaded with heavily armed NPD officers.

"That is Mr. Thomas' body they are taking to the prisoners' cemetery for burial. He was hanged early this morning," people started to murmur the news. When he heard what had happened, Bondawaa ran back into his room, fell on the ground, and began to ask himself whether it was Mr. Thomas' ghost that had just visited him, or if the encounter was a dream.

CHAPTER TWENTY-THREE

Three Years after Keifa Left for the US

Keifa had been in the United States for three years now and had written to Bondawaa only once. One day, worried that Keifa might not keep his promise to buy his ticket to America, Bondawaa began to brood over the deteriorating conditions in the Republic of Simbeck. He thought of the high cost of living, which was skyrocketing by the day, and the astronomical cost of education. He lamented the fact that government offered very few scholarships; and even those were not meant for the needy, but for the sons and daughters of those who were already well to do.

As he pondered, Bondawaa rose from the chair and walked out of the classroom. He began to pace the long corridor that stretched in front of the three classrooms on the right wing of the U-shaped building. As he paced, he recalled how only a decade ago someone on the lowest income had enough to pay rent, feed his family and the privilege of at least sitting at a palm wine bar to refresh himself. He could not understand why the situation had deteriorated so quickly that wages at whatever level had become inadequate. "Today, the monthly income of the highest paid civil servant cannot feed his family for even a week. Simbeck is now in a situation wherein most people barely survive, while few others live in affluence. Some eat once a day, whilst others eat four times a day and spend their annual vacations in Paris,

150

London, the US, or other first world countries. While there are also those who sit in strategic places in the cities to beg for their daily living," Bondawaa began to think aloud. "There is a saying that the elephant is never tired of carrying its tusk. Yes, that is quite true. But if the conditions of living in Simbeck were an elephant tusk, one would say that it is unusually large, and deliberately designed to over burden or kill the elephant. In Simbeck, living has become a magic," Bondawaa went on.

This magic of living has had an adverse repercussion on development in Simbeck. Because the average Simbeckian cannot live on his income, he goes out of his way to make ends meet. Many Simbeckians in government service siphon state funds into their private coffers; others sell state property and pocket the money; some stay away from work during official working hours doing *Mammy Coker* (moonlighting to bring in extra income) and return there only to collect their pay packets; some shamelessly solicit and receive bribes for official duties, with impunity. What is more, all these acts have been institutionalized under the maxim "A cow grazes where it is tethered." With this maxim cows were found grazing everywhere, on people's farms, on state farms, in vegetable gardens, in the national treasury, everywhere!

One day Bondawaa had cause to challenge the lackadaisical attitude of staff in the ministry in charge of Adolescent Affairs. He had gone there three times a day for five days in one week in search of some information. His persistence annoyed everyone in the ministry, and some had already engaged him in various forms of palaver, including even the Adolescent Affairs boss. Bondawaa was now regarded as a pariah by the staff of that ministry; therefore, each time he was seen there they would murmur, "The proud and arrogant fellow has come again to disrupt our work." As a matter of fact, each time Bondawaa got to that office, he would meet the staff idling. He had even begun to wonder why government had put them there, using the poor taxpayers' money to pay their wages every month for doing virtually nothing.

Most of the time, when Bondawaa had come to this ministry, the Adolescent Affairs boss was not at his desk, and nobody would look for the files to fish out the information he wanted, even when they could do so without side-stepping bureaucratic orders. They were behaving in that way deliberately. Bondawaa wanted that piece of information, and he was determined to get it without feeding any file. On the fourth day when he came back to the ministry, one of the ladies walked up to him and said, "You know what, Mr. Ndoma, I wouldn't mind searching for the file containing the information you want, but you can see the shelves are all dusty in this office. If you can only provide money for soap for me to wash my hands after I have fetched the file, why will I not help you?" She was looking straight in his eyes, a corpulent figure, now in her late forties. He was surprised when someone suddenly called her Miss.

"When will this one ever get married?" he asked himself. Considering the kind of protuberance

152

Bondawaa was seeing before him, he was not sure if this woman would ever attract a male partner.

"Sorry mummy, this ministry has a vote for that. Besides, you have office cleaners, why can't they dust the shelves?" he asked her.

"Behave as if you do not understand the system, you are not ready for the information yet," she responded angrily and bellowing, she went back to her seat. When Bondawaa visited the office again on the fifth day, he spoke to nobody but wrote a four foolscap-page letter to the Adolescent Affairs boss and left it on his table. The letter was a compendium of all that he felt about his attitude to work and those of his junior staff.

On the sixth day, now in the second week, Bondawaa was in the office again. It was 10:00 am and the Adolescent Affairs boss was at his desk, all set to swallow him up. But he was a human being like Bondawaa, and worst for him, despite the high position he was holding, he could not express himself properly. Because of this deficiency, he was very aggressive to Bondawaa. At a particular point in the row, he had with Bondawaa, he threw himself at him, but Bondawaa jumped aside and stood there laughing at the Adolescent Affairs boss derisively. However, before he left the Adolescent Affairs boss' office that morning, he had got the information he had been seeking for more than a week, and the Adolescent Affairs boss and he were already friends. Ironically, Bondawaa left the office feeling overjoyed.

"I myself have started getting the right connections," he said to himself as he went down the stairs.

CHAPTER TWENTY-FOUR

Sir Benga Advanced Teachers College

While he waited for Keifa to settle down in the US, Bondawaa entered Sir Benga Advanced Teachers College (SBATC) in Gracetown. That year, three of them matriculated for that college from Ngawobu High: Lappia, Moisia and he. They were a tough and happy trio in the college. Lappia and Moisia were reading the Sciences and Bondawaa the Arts. In addition to their areas of specialty, they read the necessary education subjects: Psychology of Education, Principles of Education, History of Simbeck Education, Methods of Education, Basic Mathematics, etc., etc.

They each had their favourite among the education subjects and those they disliked or feared. Bondawaa was the entire opposite of Lappia. He hated Educational Psychology and loved Principles of Education, but Lappia was easily the best student of Educational Psychology in their year. They therefore called him E. Stone, the author of An Introduction to Educational Psychology. But this young man dreaded Principles of Education as if it were a wolf. He said that the subject was too wordy for his comfort. Being a brilliant student, he never failed it, though he never felt at home with it. No! He never did! Moisia was the champion of Methods of Education, but he did not like History of Simbeck Education. He found it disjointed and dominated by colonial influence.

155

Academic work at SBATC was actual slavery. The trio's consolation was the beautiful location of the college. The college itself was suavely constructed and located on a flat land some two hundred yards away from the Atlantic Ocean.

At night, the sea breeze would suffuse the compound making the atmosphere there cool, pampering, and romantic; a sharp contrast with the hellish one in the heart of Gracetown. The rushing and splashing of the sea on the shore used to punctuate the silence that would dawn on the campus at night. At early dawn the campus would be shrouded in mist and the sun would slowly show its face above the thick greenish woods, and the fervour of academic work would commence. For some who were still not able to get a grip on their work, it was bravado mixed with insecurity. Bu all students mixed freely and enjoyed the fresh air that always escaped from the sea and took refuge on the campus.

The dining-hall was where all the students had their fill, but it was the most dreaded place for every student on campus, be you a fresher, finalist, or the Student Union President. It was in the dining-hall that students were corrected of their vices through a practice known as cartooning. Because of the presence of students who did fine arts as a specialist course at SBATC, cartooning was very effective there.

Exactly one month after Bondawaa and other students had joined the college as freshmen and women, the tradition of cartooning was made stark naked to them. One of their colleagues, a freshman, was cartooned. He was said to be flippant, arrogant,

156

and conceited since he entered SBATC, and sometimes behaved as if he were a lecturer.

Cartooning was normally done during dinner. If this exercise was going to be carried out one could sense it well before it took place. The High Priest who oversaw the ceremony would adorn himself in his ceremonial gear, and the dining-hall would be unusually full. Those who had gone through their meals would stick around, waiting to know who that day's ceremonial lamb was going to be. It used to be a tense moment. Most students would know that somebody was going to be cartooned – but whom? They would all wait in fear to know whom a lot of humiliation would fall on.

"It might be you!"

"Maybe yes, but I am going to wait and see – perhaps it is not me, and then I'll enjoy some fun," the students would argue among themselves while they waited.

The dining-hall was full to the brim that evening. Some students had eaten long before, and did not now have a place to sit, so many stood around waiting for the much-dreaded moment. Some waited in the hall, others in the corridor. Knives and forks were knocking against plates, jaws bulging, gullets moving up and down, and music playing softly in the background to neutralize the tension. The High Priest entered, looked around owlishly and then blew his whistle. A chart soon appeared on the notice board at the helm of the dining-hall, bearing the exact portrait of one of the freshmen. It was a plump, stocky-looking fellow in his mid-thirties. He was ridiculously portrayed. His mouth was large with thick lips, his stomach quite heavy, his eyes sticking out of their orbits and his teeth large and decayed. It was a caricature. The portrait was labelled Babu, meaning ugly. From that day on, most students have only known the victim as Babu, and he did not ever reject that name.

Spoons clattered on the tables for Babu, he was booed; water was sprinkled on his head, and some poured it into his plate. A song was spontaneously composed about him. He was brave, that Babu fellow. Amidst all that jeering he sat munching quietly. But when he got up to move out, it was another story. The taunting, clapping, booing, and rancour intensified. He lost his courage, and his legs began to tremble visibly, but he managed to walk out.

At SABTC, Bondawaa survived entirely on the student allowance of 50 Dabras he got every term as part of his bursary. It was out of this amount that he bought his toiletries, clothing, and paid his fare to and from vacation. For some students at SABTC, life was a luxury. In addition to their bursaries, their parents gave them monthly allowances and provided their basic needs, but for most, it was a period of economic and academic struggle.

Bondawaa was receiving higher education quite all right, but this meant a setback for his younger brother who was already in secondary school. The pact between Bondawaa and his father when he left form five was for him to pay for this young man to complete secondary education, before pursuing any higher education programme. But this brother's case was an unfortunate one. For two years Bondawaa had worked as a pupil teacher to pay his fees, and for all the two years he had repeated the same form. Consequently, Bondawaa had to do one of two things: To allow his brother to waste his own time and Bondawaa's, or to keep his brother out of the way so that he could equip himself well enough through higher education to properly cope with the huge task that lay ahead of him. The task to help other younger brothers and sisters, nephews, and nieces, to go through formal education.

A good number of people with provincial background in Simbeck who had had formal education even up to university level had done so either through the auspices of an elder brother, cousin, and uncle or through a mentor. But this form of assistance was now becoming cumbersome because of the weak economy of Simbeck, and the seed of individualism sown there by the forces of modernization. The consequence of this new system was that those who willingly extended such support to members of their extended families were no longer able to continue their benevolence, thus leaving the would-be beneficiaries in the darkness of illiteracy and ignorance.

Lappia and Moisia were first-rate students, and they had always been since the trio was in primary and secondary school together. Their magic, however, was hard work. They combined intelligence with hard work.

At SABTC, Lappia and Moisia read the same subjects. Each wanted to top their class. They read competitively. Bondawaa joined this competition only when it came to the education subjects. Here, they beat each other in their favourite subjects. They were one another's private tutors in these subjects. There is a lot to say about Lappia's academic passion. He was an academic gourmet, a real glutton at it. In form three, when he and Bondawaa were study partners, Bondawaa found him extraordinarily hardworking. He would sleep and wake and Lappia would still be up reading. He would sleep and wake the second time and Lappia would still be up trying to commit his entire notes to memory. He was very good at memorizing.

Lappia and Bondawaa were preparing for a geography examination one night. Their teacher was very fond of objective type of questions. The teacher had already advised them to prepare themselves for one hundred such questions. Lappia had vowed to Bondawaa that he would not miss any of them. It was already three o'clock in the morning when Bondawaa woke up for the third time, and Lappia was still reading.

"How will I get him to go to bed?" Bondawaa began to think hard. He called for a quick revision and Lappia accepted, ready to show how well prepared he was for the examination.

"What is the capital of Africa, Lappia?" He asked.

"Nairobi".

"No".

"Accra".

"No".

"Oh Jesus, I read it just now. Please just a minute. It will soon come," he begged for time, tapping his forehead gently.

"You mean London?"

"Nope, you are going too far away."

"Oh yes, it is Addis Ababa."

"But look Lappia; has any Geography teacher ever taught you about the capital of Africa?" He felt frustrated, packed all his books, and went to bed shaking his head vaguely.

In form five they nicknamed Lappia, Theophilus. Though a science student, he offered Bible Knowledge for the General Certificate of Education at the Ordinary Level. Answering a context question in one of the tests they used to have on that subject, Lappia started off thus, "In the first book O Theophilus, I have dealt with all that Jesus began to do and teach (Acts 1.1)." You see, Lappia did not need to write all of this, but he had already crammed all of it and wanted to gain more marks. He thought by writing everything he had committed to memory from that chapter would give him an advantage over the other pupils. Their teacher, a pleasant Indian woman, laughed so hard that she cried.

During their days at SABTC, Bondawaa was in the library one day when a friend came looking for him. "You are urgently needed in the dormitory, your brother Lappia has gone bananas." Bondawaa merely smiled at the friend and dismissed the whole idea as foolish, because he knew exactly what was going on. The most crucial examinations at SABTC were the intermediate examinations which students took in the second year. Any student who failed even one subject was sent out of the college. Lappia was never the type to fail examinations such as those, but he had overworked himself for them. One evening, as he sat in his room trying to regurgitate some of the notes he had crammed, nothing came. Out of fatigue, his mind went blank. He panicked and began to weep and behave abnormally. By the time Bondawaa entered the room Lappia had packed his books and was packing his clothes to go home.

"Lappia, what are you doing?" Bondawaa asked.

"Going home, Bondawaa, there is nothing in my head for this crucial examination ahead of us," he said in tears.

"You need to put something there Lappia, but you are not going home because you have nothing convincing to tell anybody when you get there." The room became very quiet, and Lappia sat restlessly, wiping tears from his eyes with the back of his hand. When Bondawaa looked at him again, he was reminded of the time they were growing up. Lappia was a spoilt child who would cry for hours without end for no good reason.

Lappia and Bondawaa went to Langua Beach that evening to watch the fishermen return from sea with their catch. It was about a mile and a half's journey from the campus. Walking from campus to this beach was always consolatory. One would first walk through half a mile stretch of bush before one got to a community of fishermen and their families; the community sprawled right down to the beach. Walking the half-mile distance through the bush always brought Bondawaa a feeling of nostalgia. The birds singing competitively in the undergrowth, each one trying to excel in a gratuitous melody show. The nightingale would sing and come closer to the road if someone was whistling the exact sounds it was making. It would sit at a close range and display its beautiful feathers. The squirrels would cross the road in front of you with their beautiful tails. There is a belief among Bondawaa's people that if a squirrel crossed the road before you from left to right when you were on a journey, you were bound to have good luck. But when it did the opposite, you were in for ill luck. While Lappia and Bondawaa were strolling leisurely that evening, a squirrel jumped on the road close to them from the left, got so frightened by their presence, that it went back into the bush in the same direction it had come. They both laughed.

"What luck does this signify?" Lappia asked still laughing.

"She may come but may not have the time to follow you to the hide-out. It is a sign of half-luck. You may see her, but not have her," Bondawaa teased Lappia.

They went in silence through the bush to Langua, the fishmongers' settlement. It was a shantytown with houses standing close to each other. The whole town was most of the time shrouded in a mass of smoke from the numerous ovens designed for smoking fish. Despite the huge quantity of fish they produced per day, some of the inhabitants of Langua were emaciated and pallid from excessive consumption of alcohol. At Langua, Lappia bought a packet of cigarettes and a box of matches. He was a heavy smoker. He never ate if he was not sure of a stick of cigarette to smoke after the food. He smoked close to a packet when he was

163

studying. When he was angered, he smoked ceaselessly. Lappia was reticent and believed very much in action. If he got angry, the only way he would calm himself down was to smoke and smoke and smoke.

When they got to Langua Beach the horizon was shimmering in the reddish flakes of the setting sun. The last batch of fishermen was returning, some with a huge catch, and some with little. They would always come back looking exhausted. People would rush at them and help them unload their boats and haggling would begin. Children between the ages of five and ten years would mischievously sneak between people's legs, snatch fishes, slip them into their pockets or shirts and disappear into the crowd.

The vultures would wait patiently in the coconut trees to take care of the unwanted catch after everyone had gone away. The pelicans would fly past in large numbers, anxious to avoid night creeping in to take over from the sun. The sun would get bigger and bigger and redder and redder, before finally escaping into the bosom of the horizon.

Langua Beach was the centre of activities every blessed evening except on Sundays when the fishermen usually take a break. There was a large crowd when Lappia and Bondawaa got there. But for Lappia the beach was still not full yet. Theresa, the main purpose for their stroll, had still not arrived. They waited and waited, enjoying the scenery. Intermittently, the sound of revolutionary music would invade them from a pub, swallowing all other sounds – even the hoarse noise with which the sea would rush onto the bank. The crowd began to dwindle. The music was now getting regular and the wind cooler and cooler. Yet, Theresa did not appear.

"What luck did the half-crossing from the left by the squirrel symbolize?" Bondawaa asked Lappia.

"You can interpret it better, Bondawaa. Why not have some beers at the pub?" Lappia asked in disappointment.

CHAPTER TWENTY-FIVE

Benevolent Believers Secondary School

Bondawaa had been teaching at Benevolent Believers Secondary School (BBSS) since he completed the Advanced Teachers Certificate course at SBATC. Moisia taught at the Beinke Secondary School for Girls in Yamalu, in the South of Simbeck. Beinke was one of the first secondary schools for girls to be founded upcountry, and it was renowned for the quality of women it turned out, morally as well as academically. Bondawaa thought it was all a joke when Moisia brought a Teachers Dossier one day and told him he was filling it in for Beinke.

"No, this is for Lappia, just give it back to him," he said confidently, laughing ecstatically at the same time.

"Wait and see if it is for Lappia", Moisia said, took the form from Bondawaa and went back to his room. His room was adjacent to Bondawaa's on the last floor of Maiju Sifoi Hall. It was a massive hall, which housed more than half the population of the male students on campus.

Teachers at secondary schools for girls were mostly females. Male teachers joined them only to teach subjects that were not popular among female teachers such as Mathematics, Physics, Chemistry and Agriculture. Any male teacher employed to teach in a girls school must first be married and have children.

166

BBSS was steadily gaining popularity among the schools in Gracetown. Though it was a relatively young school, it was the champion in everything – football, Ordinary and Advanced Level General Certificate examinations, discipline – you name it! The magic behind their success was very simple – mass intake of pupils. The philosophy of the principal was that wherever there was a large population of people, there was bound to be the extreme of all the qualities, and that the leader's task was to relentlessly harness and cultivate whatever was good in them and then suppress the bad. That was how they excelled at BBSS!

In Ngawobu High, the secondary school Bondawaa attended, the total population never exceeded four hundred at any given time. The teacher-pupil ratio was always conducive to learning, at its worst one teacher to thirty-five pupils. In Ngawobu High, the teacher knew each pupil in his class by name, voice, handwriting, and even by the shadow. Pupils therefore found it extremely difficult to hoodwink their teachers.

It was an entirely different situation in Believers Benevolent Secondary School, which was nicknamed United Nations. It had not less than four thousand pupils every academic year. At that time, it was the school with the largest number of pupils in the whole of Simbeck. The pupil-teacher ratio was appalling, one to ninety at least. The classrooms were always cramped with seats, stuffy and with very poor acoustics. It was even worse if you were teaching one of the compulsory subjects: English, Mathematics and Biology to a class of form five. You would not have less than two hundred pupils in any of these classes. The school presented at least five hundred candidates for the GCE 'O' Level examinations; a number far more than the total enrolment of most secondary schools in the provincial towns. At BBSS, there were over seventy-five members of the teaching staff. The staffroom was far too small to accommodate all of them. When it was full, some of them found sitting accommodation in the school's canteen or the library. Others sat in the biology, the physics, or the chemistry laboratories.

CHAPTER TWENTY-SIX

Life after University

After university, Bondawaa's life became miserable every now and then. His situation was not made difficult entirely by the chaotic economic situation in Simbeck, but by the extended family responsibilities that had been placed firmly on his head. As time progressed, Bondawaa began to understand that it takes more than formal education to build the kind of family he had envisioned. That sacrificing himself for the growth of the Ndoma family was not enough. Already, his own growth was being retarded by his attempt to rear a forest of giant trees. What was going on was stunted growth. "Human development is a gradual process. A firm foundation needed to have been laid long before now, upon which to build an ambitious human development programme," he said to himself one day. But even as he said this, Bondawaa knew he was now too enmeshed in this process to allow it to crumble. "I may not have made a recognizable impact yet, but there is now some foundation upon which the younger and ambitious generation of the Ndomas may build," he said.

Bondawaa walked into the office of the Vice-Principal of Ngawobu High one Wednesday morning. He had gone there to seek admission for one of his younger brothers who had lost his place at one of the best secondary schools in Kwabu. Mama Davies had been Vice-Principal for a long time. Even while Bondawaa was a pupil, twelve years ago. A meticulous and dutiful woman, Mama Davies, now burdened with age, was still the miracle behind the success of the school, even in the face of challenging problems plaguing the school administration.

As he entered the office, an inscription hanging on the wall over Mama Davies' chair caught Bondawaa's eye. The inscription read: "No one can make you better than yourself." He was stunned but tried not to show it. Juma was a brilliant brat. Bondawaa therefore saw no reason why he should not nurture that brilliance in him until it sprouted into a giant tree. Of course, a good shade is meant for all who travel that road. As soon as the admission was fixed, Bondawaa raised his head up and asked Mama Davies, "What do you mean by that inscription over your head?"

"Oh, it speaks for itself, Bondawaa. The inscription is self-explanatory," she said, and lavished a motherly smile on him.

"I am surprised that an inscription such as that should be hanging in the office of a school administrator. The teacher, to my mind, defies that inscription. You teachers are the architects of all the lawyers, bank managers, doctors, engineers, university lecturers, presidents, and ministers – all the prominent people of the world and yet, you are mere teachers. What about that?" Bondawaa philosophized.

"At the same time, Bondawaa, some of the worst criminals go through teachers. We merely wake up these professions in them. If these qualities are not fast asleep in the children, they wake up as soon as we tap on their doors. That is what this inscription is saying. If, for example, your brother here does not allow his talent to over-sleep, it will be all the better for him." She gave Bondawaa another mesmerizing smile after this ingenious interpretation. Memories of her as his Mathematics and Physics teacher came back to him fresh,

"What about the criminals who pass through you?" Bondawaa persisted. She sat there and looked at him for a brief while. The office became quiet and enormous. As he looked at her fully in the face now, he realized she had grown several years older than she was when he was there in the school as a pupil. When she smiled again, her face wore several wrinkles.

"Oh, having passed through us yourself you know what we do with them." With very little effort, she got up from her seat, walked to the window very slowly and began to look across the vast school compound.

"I have served this school from the very first day it was founded. That is twenty-four good years now, Bondawaa, and since that time we've had good and bad pupils pass through the doors of this Christian institution. We have always, through the guidance of the Lord Almighty, tried our best to nurture the varied positive talents of our pupils and to correct their vices."

"I know teachers can perform wonders if they are determined," he said, shook her fragile hand gently and walked out of the office.

Halfway through that academic year, Sombo, Bondawaa's half-sister who was in form four, got pregnant. The news struck him like a thunderbolt. For three nights he could not sleep. Each time he wanted to sleep; he could see heinous objects running after him. He drank heavily all those days, but that did not help. Suddenly, one day, his encounter with Tonya, the young call girl with whom they were locked up in the room, came to his mind; he lost consciousness and crashed on the ground.

When Bondawaa came round, he sent to call Sombo. She arrived two days later, in a very independent mood.

"I will return to Ngawobu tomorrow *Ngɔ* Bondawaa," Sombo said as she sank into the chair after she had put her bag in the guest room.

"You are no longer going to school, why are you in such a hurry to go back? And as a matter of fact, I have not even told you why I called you here, have I?" Bondawaa asked her a little sternly.

Oh, I must go back to the one whose child I am carrying in my womb. He wants me back tomorrow. We love each other so much. I cannot afford to be away from him for even two nights," she said and frowned her face at him.

"But when did you start talking to me like this, Sombo?" Bondawaa asked, almost shouting. She ran to him, wrapped her arms around him and began to say in tears, "Can't you see that I am already four months pregnant. Are you ever going to continue treating me like a child?" Bondawaa recoiled from her and began

172

to pace the parlour restlessly, whistling, his eyes red like an angry, spitting cobra's.

"But can't you see that you have shamed the family?" Bondawaa said, trembling physically after he had had some composure. She prostrated to him and attempted to explain,
"But, but, but..."

"Do our parents know about this pregnancy?" Bondawaa interrupted her.

"Of course, my husband has been home to dad and mom twice. Each time he had been there, he had taken with him handsome gifts for them. They like and appreciate him," she said.

"Please stop calling him your husband. He is a predator, an interloper, an enemy of, of..." He was now struggling for words. "You should have nothing to do with him from today."

"He is my husband. I am already carrying his child in my womb!" she said defiantly.

"I have called you here to abort your so-called child. You must complete your schooling. You are too small and ill prepared to be somebody's wife, and to carry a child. The ending will be disastrous for you," Bondawaa said firmly.

"I don't want school to make a crone of me before I join my husband. He must have me now that I am young, fresh, and attractive!"

"Yes, when you are inexperienced and defenceless, so that it will be easy for him to use and dump you," Bondawaa said, with his teeth clenched.

"Our parents will not forgive you for such a murderous thought, Ngɔ Bondawaa; you know that too well."

"How will they know?"

"They know about the pregnancy already, I have said. They are now watching its growth. You should know that!"

"Don't you want to be a professional woman, highly educated and a bread winner?"

"We cannot all earn our fortunes through schooling. You must stop making this mistake. We have our different destinies. You cannot change our destinies overnight."

"Sombo, what I am doing is trying to help the budding generation of the Ndoma family to have control over their destinies," Bondawaa said, feeling dejected and helpless.

Suddenly, Sombo became hysterical and fainted; Bondawaa ran out in search of a taxi to take her to hospital.

Bondawaa's experience in the office of the Vice Principal of Ngawobu High, and his encounter with Sombo magnified the ramifications of his vision. It now dawned on him that he was faced with a formidable task, with which he was not making much progress. The trees were not growing, and his dream of a forest of giant trees started to evaporate. This reality put him at war with himself. He began to drink heavily and dreaded going home any more to face his parents.

One afternoon Bondawaa set out for a supermarket to buy one or two cartons of can beer to replenish the stock he had at home. As he walked the distance from the bus stop to the supermarket, he began to talk to himself unconsciously: "Bondawaa, what happened to all the eighteen-year-old trees growing in your forest?"

"Oh, they were ravaged by a logger who went there surreptitiously. By the time we realised, they had all gone." "What happened to the seventeen-year-olds?"

"Oh, if you can remember the storm of last year, it pummelled every big tree there."
"And the sixteen-year-olds?"
"Bush fire, malicious bush fire set by destructive youth."
"How about the forester himself, can he ever grow taller?" "Please-e-e!"
While he walked along the street talking to himself in a delirium, Bondawaa collided with a gorgeously dressed young woman and they both crashed on the ground.

"Stupid addict, the Lord will build your house in hell," she cursed as she got up, dusted herself and hurried away.
"Any bruises?" Bondawaa yelled after her.

"Please blame the system for driving some of its citizen crazy," a young man joked after her, laughing. From that day on, Bondawaa started to ponder the futility of his dream of rearing a forest of giant trees.

There is a saying that only God and fools do not change. But which of the systems flourishes under the current climate: the "we" or the "I"? Now as Bondawaa examines the climate of yesterday and that of today, he begins to understand the reasons why most farmers who stubbornly cultivate the "we" seed are doomed to have a low harvest as compared to those who grow the "I" seed. A lot has gone wrong with the climate. Today, the tropical climate has been infiltrated by the temperate climate, making the growth of the "we" seed difficult. Today, the people accept western values *en bloc*; they eat the fish for the protein without guarding themselves against the bones.

As Bondawaa got to the watershed of his determination to carry every member of the Ndoma family on his shoulder, the warning of his late granddad kept on ringing in his ears. "The new virus, individualism, must not be allowed to breed in your heart. It is destroying our communities."

However, his dream of several giant trees growing in the Ndoma forest-family began to take on a new form. While one tree cannot make a forest, no forest has trees that are all equal. "Help everyone to grow according to his or her capability. Those whose giant trees are not fast asleep will certainly grow to the top. Bondawaa there and then resolved to pursue higher education. The tallest tree advertises the forest. The taller it is, the farther away the forest can be seen," he gave reasons for his new plan. "Nurture willing potential giant trees to grow tall and tall and your forest can be seen from afar. Better still, there should always be the biggest and tallest tree, the cotton tree that God Himself has blessed," Bondawaa resolved.

CHAPTER TWENTY-SEVEN

Six Years after Keifa's been Gone

Keifa was now in his sixth year in the United States of America. He was doing a master's programme in Sociology, one of the few fortunate products of Ngawobu High to be doing a post-graduate degree. Bondawaa had almost given up on him when his letter came in on one foggy day. The wind was blowing aggressively from Mount Gabriel, sweeping across the parlour, forcing the windows to close with big bangs, and lifting hangings from the walls and bringing them to crash on the floor. Sparrows were being tossed up and down by this unusually violent wind. The vultures sat in cotton trees and wrapped themselves with their overlying wings. It was one of those severe winds that occasionally visited Gracetown during the harmattan.

> *"Hope you have been saving some money towards coming to the US to study.*
> *I am ready to pay one-third of the cost of your flight,"* the letter read.

Bondawaa looked dimly into it, his lips parted. He was never sure if he was smiling, or he was never able to keep his lips together again. His hands were now trembling visibly, and sweat was dropping down his fingertips, despite the dry harmattan wind that was blowing viciously. Holding the letter firmly, he began to murmur to himself, "What an arduous task has this man put on me, in a country where even food to eat is

177

hard to get for most families, including a poor teacher like me?"

Bondawaa began to recall how Keifa, and he had saved copiously seven years before in vain to buy an air ticket for one of them to travel to the US. His earning power had increased four times, but he had not been able to beat the inflation, and his responsibility had quadrupled. He accepted the challenge. "I'll try, he will surely not beat me on this", he said. As he was folding the letter to put it away, the wind blew it from his hand and unfortunately, it landed into the gutter. Before Bondawaa could reach it, the letter had been soiled beyond recognition. As he bowed down to pick it, the stench from the gutter hit him hard and at once, he began to spew. He ran into the toilet, puked a while, took hot showers and went straight to bed.

That very year, Bondawaa had joined a thrift organized in their school. It comprised ten members, each contributing one hundred Dabras a month. When it was the turn of a member, he or she collected nine hundred Dabras, aside from the recipient's monthly salary. Before now, Bondawaa's main dream of joining the thrift was to raise money to buy a refrigerator and some furniture. But to use it now as part payment for an air ticket to the US was even a more profitable venture. Bondawaa was prepared to use every genuine means that would get him to America. Though it was gradually becoming clear that Keifa, the friend he had adored all along, was about to make things stiff for him, he was never going to relent. As the economy of Simbeck continued to fall and government's subsidy for higher education grew thinner, the United States of

America became the greener pasture for many young Simbeckians who wanted to develop themselves and their families. Every Christmas, Simbeckians living in the US would come home looking affluent, contrasting sharply with their starving brothers and sisters back at home.

Keifa asked a University in New Jersey to send Bondawaa an application form for an undergraduate programme in the Humanities. When the college eventually sent one, Bondawaa's heart glowed. In his mind's eye, he began to see himself on the road to achieving his dream. His Test of English as a Foreign Language (TOEFL) result was quite good, and he was soon offered a place at the New Jersey University for the Humanities. After he had received his acceptance letter, Bondawaa got his passport ready and was now waiting for the part-payment for his ticket to come from Keifa. Bondawaa will then appear for the visa interview and will, God willing, fly all the way to the US and join Keifa.

Two months passed without a single line from Keifa. Bondawaa wrote and wrote to him, but there was no response. In the fourth week of the third month of waiting, Keifa wrote. It was a longish letter containing all the rhetoric of the world. He wrote that he was convinced there was a friend of his who needed help more urgently than Bondawaa. Part of the letter read:

"... Bondawaa, I know that with the Advanced Teachers Certificate on your back, your position is much better than Dugbah's, who is unemployed.

179

Let him come to the US first; he will later secure a
ticket for you to follow…"

As Bondawaa finished reading this portion, tears
filled his eyes. They were streaming down his cheeks
into his mouth; hot, sticky, and salty. As the tears dried
up, he saw the road to his ambition wrapped up in
thorns, vipers and wasps keeping guard on it. "I'll
remain here in my home-country and be educated to
the highest degree that my university can offer. If ever
I must go to the US to study, it will have to be on a
scholarship, not through a friend who has failed me
calamitously," Bondawaa resolved very strongly, and
let out a sardonic laugh loud enough to warrant people
to come asking what was going on.

*****

Dugbah's air ticket reached Bondawaa by post with
a very short covering note:

Dear Bondawaa,
Please take this ticket to Dugbah at Ngawobu and tell
him he is expected in the US on November 8. Kindly
ask him to send a cablegram and confirm if he can
make it on this date, so that I'll meet him at the JFK
Airport in New York.
Please be good.
Your brother,
Keifa.

180

Bondawaa's hands trembled as he held the covering note in his right hand, and the ticket in the left. "Does he still continue to trust and call me his brother after all this, or is he trying to ridicule me?" he asked himself. He was now sweating profusely and suddenly realized that he was hungry. But he had no appetite and desire to eat.

After he had looked at the letter and the air ticket thoroughly for the second time, Bondawaa began to toy with the idea of converting it to his own use, but soon gave up. He was not the stuff for a practice such as that. He sent a telegram to Dugbah asking him to travel to Gracetown ready to fly to the United States. He arrived the next day. Bondawaa helped him to obtain a passport, visa, and a yellow card, and saw him off at the airport. When the plane took off with Dugbah on board, Bondawaa recalled the day he saw Keifa off at the same airport some seven years ago. The scenery was the same; the tall palm trees towered over the greenish undergrowth. The bluish sea rippling by, on which fishing vessels of varied make navigated. The sky was wrapped in dark cloud with the rain falling aggressively on the tarmac.

Before he left for the plane, Keifa had whispered in Bondawaa's ears, "Be rest assured that I will send an air ticket for you to join me, and soon." And now it was Dugbah's turn to make the same promise to him, a bloody fool who had never had a stroke of luck to board a plane to even a neighbouring African country. Bondawaa stood dazed as the plane flew nose right up. He began to imagine how the passengers would maintain their balance when the plane is flying head up and tail down.

CHAPTER TWENTY-EIGHT

Keifa's Return

Keifa returned from the United States of America with a Master of Arts degree in Sociology, and took up appointment at Ngawobu High, his alma mater, as a teacher. Many people lauded his initiative, the first ex-pupil to return to his school with such a prestigious degree to teach. Keifa arrived in Ngawobu close to Christmas. Posters advertising entertainments in Ngawobu and the surroundings carried his name as Master of Ceremonies (MC). The occasions were all jammed packed, people attended mainly to see and listen to the MC, Keifa Seppeh-Bengeh, BA, MA, Dip. Ed. What was more, all these certificates were obtained from some of the top-notch universities in the US. Most of the time, Keifa talked through his nostrils, revelling in an indiscriminate use of longwinded sociological jargons. His style accorded him a lot of applause.

"The guy is fantastic; he should not have come back to Simbeck. How much are they going to pay him for this plenty book in his head?" a young woman asked.

"I think the man should go to Bombay College, University of Simbeck and lecture, here at Ngawobu High he would be talking above his pupils," the same woman said, clapping and hopping in admiration of Keifa.

183

"Yes, he should go and speak his -isms at the university, not here," a young man standing by the lady full of admiration for Keifa said sarcastically.

"I think he has started from the right beginning. Teaching here will help him to understand the needs and aspirations of his people. It will create a situation for him to interact with his people better and to represent them well in Parliament," an elder observed.

"Ha, ha, ha; Papa, please don't make me laugh. You know we have a good number of teachers in our House of Representatives, and with all that, they cannot even improve the living conditions of their fellow teachers," another young man remarked, laughing impertinently.

"Yes o, they say that soap cannot wash its own clothes," the elder changed his mind and he and the young man burst out laughing excitedly.

On December 23 Bondawaa went to Ngawobu for Christmas vacation. Keifa had arrived there two weeks earlier. He was surprised to learn that Keifa had come back home for good, because he had told Bondawaa that when Dugbah joined him in the U S, he would make sure that they both work hard together to send him an air ticket. And now when he arrived in Ngawobu there was this wild news going all around that one of the soil's most educated children had come back home from overseas; Keifa Seppeh-Bengeh; the man everyone acclaims speaks English even better than the native speakers of the language.

On the evening of Bondawaa's arrival at Ngawobu, Keifa went straight to his house to meet him. He was

184

two times larger than he was when he left Simbeck and was much smarter. What Bondawaa did not like about Keifa's appearance was that he was now partially bald, and his hair and beard had grey strands all over. His teeth had lost their African whiteness. He embraced Bondawaa with pretentious warmness, but Bondawaa's own emotion had momentarily crossed the bridge of affectation. He was genuinely cold and shivering with regret and disappointment. His reaction stabbed Keifa like a poisonous dagger.

"Bondawaa, I know that standing before you this very moment is real audacity on my part. Please let us discuss my behaviour later. Right now, my head is spinning with remorse," Keifa said and sighed.

"But you are not my God, it was all out of love and mistake that I expected you to make me in your own image," Bondawaa said, laughed cynically and asked Keifa to take a seat. As he sat dawn, Keifa looked physically uneasy, but Bondawaa was much composed.

"Bondawaa, can we please talk about your study programme in the US sometime after Christmas? All is not lost yet, with Dugbah over there," Keifa said almost gasping.

"Breaking a bird's eggs does not stop its procreation, but cutting off its genitals does. Keifa, from now on I will take care of my own study programmes, be they in London," Bondawaa relieved Keifa of his worries in a strong language. A sombre silence filled the room and both men sat there avoiding each other's eye.

In less than six months of his arrival, Keifa's popularity began to raise an alarm, and the Parliamentary Representative of their constituency became jittery. For politicians all over Simbeck, any progressive and popular person in their constituency who does not go directly and pledge his or her loyalty to them is considered a threat. Rumours started going round that Keifa had political ambition. That he was only using teaching as a stepping-stone to his heart's desire.

Keifa progressed rapidly at Ngawobu High, but he was in every respect, one that had been heavily acculturated. As a nephew of the late Bengeh, the once successful businessman now returned from overseas with a string of certificates, a lot of deflated members and protégés of the Bengeh family hoped that they would bubble up again through him. Every evening the elders, most of them friends and relations of his late uncle would pay courtesy calls on him. They would come with varied requests and complaints.

"My child, my mouth has gone without even a pinch of snuff for days," this elder would say.

"Our sunshine, I have only rags for my clothing," another would say.

"Our greatest child, food is the major problem for us the aged. All these wrinkles you see on our faces and bodies are caused by constant hunger. Age has little to do with them," some would complain. Keifa would only tell them that he was writing down all their complaints in a book for onward submission to some humanitarians where he had come from. At first the people took him seriously, and therefore, their complaints multiplied. Issues like bush dispute, bride price, lack of school fees, inflation, etc., were added to the list.

Six months passed, one year, two years and there was still no reaction from the humanitarians. One day the people made a bold move by asking Keifa to send a letter of reminder to the humanitarians. Keifa took offence and left his uncle's compound where he had been living since he returned from the US, for staff quarters on the school campus. Before Keifa left, he summoned his relatives to a general family meeting at which he explained the reasons for relocating to the school quarters. He said he wanted privacy and an atmosphere conducive to bringing up his children the way he wanted.

"It will save both parties embarrassment if people made appointments before they visited me on the campus," Keifa warned.

"How about your children, should we ask permission before we see them, our own grandchildren?" one of his aunts asked, furious.

"I mean no one should go to our house to see any of us without making an appointment. Before they became your grandchildren, they became my children first. I'm going to rear fierce dogs at my new residence. The white man says warning before wounding," Keifa told his people light-heartedly.

"We would want you to take some of your cousins and your ailing uncle to live there with you. When you do that, no one of us will bother you any longer," one of his brothers said bravely. Keifa could not control his anger after this seemingly unreasonable request.

"You all had something to eat and wear when I was away, why should your food, clothing, snuff, school fees and other wants be my responsibility now?"

"Don't you know what a child is for, my boy, especially a successful child? Don't you know? If you have nothing to give us, don't insult us. We are your parents," the eldest of his uncles said, visibly angry.

"I agree, but your unreasonable demands will only make me and my family live below our status. It will be ridiculous," Keifa said. When the meeting broke off, most of the family members were baffled by their son's outright refusal to take up responsibility for them and the rest of the extended family members.

As Keifa estranged himself from his people, his relationship with the school authorities became stronger and stronger. Under five years he became the principal of Ngawobu High, the first black and son of the soil to hold that post. The school's affairs were always his number one priority.

"If they call you a witch your mouth should always be fastened upon the wall," he would always say to people as he went up and down the school compound. He was running the school at the expense of his domestic life and relationship with the townspeople. He left his office late and was most times late in town, all in the interest of the school. Each time his wife complained he would say he had a lot of enemies on the staff, and therefore he would not just rest on his oars at home as if all was well with him.

*****

One hot March Day, the Paramount Chief, the Chiefdom Speaker, Wards Councillors, Section Chiefs, Village Chiefs, Tribal Authorities, and other stakeholders of Ngawobu chiefdom assembled in Ngawobu town to receive the Resident Minister and his entourage. They were coming to inform the chiefdom people about the roles of the new local government in national development.

At 9:00 am prompt all the people concerned had assembled at the Chiefdom Court Barrie. The Minister and his team were expected at 11am. Singers and dancers of all kinds had gathered in the forecourt of the Barrie, the pupils had lined up the route from the bridge to the Barrie. The hammock bearers stood just in front of the bridge all set to convey the Minister from there to the Barrie. At intervals, the Paramount Chief's horn blower would add crescendo to the harmonious sounds of the musical instruments.

The high table was covered with a thick, enormous, antique country-cloth made probably at the time of the great grandfather of the current Paramount Chief. Adorned in a luxurious, floating gown, the Paramount Chief sat at the far right of the high table. His messenger in brown uniform with yellow stripes on the left and right sides of his trouser stood over him, fanning him gently. Keifa sat at the other end of the table. He wore a three-piece suit with a necktie, which was choking his throat by the minute. He sat there drenched in his own sweat, waiting to deliver the welcome address. He had longed for an occasion such

189

as this to display his academic fervour and to throw hints about his intention to represent his people in Parliament. The people waited and waited. The sun moved half-way across the town, the pupils disappeared from the route in batches, the musicians stopped playing, masked devils unmasked, the crowd in the Barrie grew thinner; yet the Minister and his team were nowhere to be seen.

There was a sudden commotion in the Barrie. The Section Chief of Kakuma had collapsed.

"Please give room, he needs fresh air!"

"Take him to the dispensary; he needs some rest, it is exhaustion!" On the way to the dispensary, Chief Ngandie died. The town was thrown into confusion. A lot of explanations were given for the sudden death of the chief. Some said that he was hypertensive, a condition that is exacerbated by heat and tension. Others claimed that he was asthmatic. The most popular explanation was that the Chief did not have enough juju on him to appear at such a public gathering.

Ngandie had only recently been made Section Chief. That was the first time he was attending a meeting comprising all the chiefs of the chiefdom. At such a mammoth meeting of chiefs, they usually test one another's manhood. Whenever such a mammoth meeting ends, there was a tendency for a lesser chief, one not thoroughly immersed in juju, to die, the popular opinion went. On a previous occasion the Paramount Chiefs and chiefdom elders of five chiefdoms had met on a small island over a bush dispute between Loyah and Ngawobu Chiefdoms.

190

Whilst they were assembled waiting for the District Commissioner to arrive, the Paramount Chief of Towahun Chiefdom collapsed and was foaming at the mouth. The Paramount Chief of Ngawobu lifted him up by the hand, shook him and said, "You should not be attending meetings of this nature if you are not seasoned enough."

As the wailing subsided, the Chiefs agreed to take the corpse to its hometown for interment. Kakuma was twenty-four miles away, so the idea of carrying the corpse in a hammock was ruled out. "There has long been a mutual relationship between the school and the community," the people said as they approached Keifa, led by the Paramount Chief to ask him for the use of the school van to convey the corpse. One would have thought that Keifa would use this opportunity, Godsend as it were, to win the confidence and support of the opinion leaders of the chiefdom for his future ambition. But he did not. He was far too principled – never ready to compromise the rules and regulations of the school for anything. As far as he was concerned, it was better to be favoured by the school authorities than by the chiefdom people. After all, the former were his employing authorities to whom he was directly answerable.

As he lay in bed that night, Keifa started to introspect. He agreed that it was not in his own interest to have refused the people the use of the school van, though it would have been illegal for him to do so. However, he took consolation in the fact that he did not compromise the principles of the school; the virtue that had rapidly brought him to the top.

191

When Ngawobu High was founded, the chiefdom people contributed immensely to its development. Through communal labour they brushed and stumped the site on which additional buildings for the school are now erected. They also constructed the football field and the lawn tennis court. The school was the baby of the Paramount Chief then. He even went out of his way to ensure that it succeeded. He asked the people of Ngawobu to house the pupils who couldn't afford to live in the boarding department, and to be nice to them. With this kind of support from the Paramount Chief and his chiefdom people for the school, there was a healthy relationship between it and the community. The school therefore grew rapidly, making much success.

Notwithstanding the rift that existed between the new leadership of the school and the community, Keifa continued to be in the good books of the school authorities. For them, he was the most progressive and the most disciplined principal in the history of the school. Even with the enrolment of the school and standards on the decline.

Being a principal in those days was like being a demigod. The post was as lucrative as it commanded dignity and respect. First, when he decided to teach in a village school with an eye on being its principal, Keifa was not convinced that he had made a good decision. But when he found himself at the top, he started to feel differently. In a short time, he became the most important personality in the chiefdom, the richest and the most powerful. He had the most expensive car and had built himself a palatial house in

Ngawobu and two in Kwabu. When he entered the staffroom or the assembly hall during devotion, everybody would rise, even his vice principal, to recognise his presence.

Most songs composed in the chiefdom carried his name. Keifa's favourite song was:

O Sama –o
Keifa beingɔ a maha jia
O Sama -o
O Sama-o
Nya nda hineimia a Keifa lɔ
O Sama-o

O Sama-o
Nya nda mahiimia a Keifa lɔ
O Sama o

O Sama-o
Keifa knows how to walk a chiefly walk
O Sama-o

O Sama-o
Keifa is my own husband
O Sama-o

O Sama-o
Keifa is my own chief
O Sama-o

The children would sing his name at play, on moonlit nights; men on the farms, and women when pounding

193

in the mortar. He became a phenomenon. He grew too big for Ngawobu High and the chiefdom and wanted to get into something bigger. A good proportion of the indigenes of Ngawobu appreciated Keifa for being on record as the only highly educated son of the soil to come and work in his own chiefdom headquarters, though it lacked all the social amenities found in the cities.

"We do not eat his money. However, his mere presence in this chiefdom is enough protection for all of us. No one will use his education and wealth to demean any son of Ngawobu, with Keifa in our midst," the people would say. Some others considered him a man filthy rich, but who kept all his money to himself. The popular saying about him, which was also composed into a song, was:

> *This Keifa has a lot of money,*
> *But he does not share it with anyone.*

When he wanted to boast, or when he had taken some alcohol and was feeling high, he would sing this song quietly to himself. Sometimes he would even play the soundtrack on his musical set and dance to it sluggishly, rubbing his hands on his pot belly.

CHAPTER TWENTY-NINE

Warning Against Individualism

Bondawaa was now working avidly towards his own self growth. He read all documents that carried adverts about foreign awards for postgraduate studies. After months of combing through newspapers, brochures in libraries, he finally applied for an award to pursue an M.A. in African Studies tenable in the United Kingdom. He had forgotten all about this application when one evening, as he sat in his favourite corner in his porch listening to the Simbeck Broadcasting Service (SBS), he heard his name aired as one of those shortlisted for the interview for the award. The night prior to the day of the interview was a sleepless one for Bondawaa. He kept imagining questions and seeking suitable answers to them.

The conference room where the interview was conducted was a massive one. Interviewers filled all the seats, arranged in a semi-circle. The single seat reserved for the interviewees was placed midway along the opening of the semi-circle.

"Good morning, ladies and gentlemen," Bondawaa greeted as he entered the hall. The acoustic was such that his voice filled the room.

"Please sit down and welcome to the interview," the Chairman said as Bondawaa stood looking at the empty chair.

"Thank you, sir", he said and sat down. To his surprise the chair was rickety and creaked as he sat on it.

"Ladies and gentlemen, do you have questions for Mr. Ndoma?" the chairman asked.

"Mr. Ndoma, how relevant is this course to your work?" a man in his mid-fifties, sitting fourth to the left of Bondawaa, asked.

"The African culture, particularly ours here in Simbeck, needs to be interpreted from our own perspective, using our own microscope to observe and interpret it, and in the most appropriate words. Our children should be encouraged to love, understand, and appreciate their culture; they should..." As Bondawaa was trying to find his feet in answering this question, the only female on the panel interrupted him. "Excuse me, Mr. Chairman," without being given the floor she went on to interject. "Mr. Ndoma, what role will you play in all this?"

"I will lead a crusade on strengthening this consciousness in the formal and the non-formal education sectors in this country; through research and documentation," he said. "Do you hope to come back if you are given the award?" "I am sure, I owe a duty to this country," he answered.

"Mr. Ndoma are you two, three, four or five man strong for this interview?" the Chairman asked.

"Sir, I am sorry I do not understand that question," Bondawaa pretended.

"Mr. Ndoma, this question is very crucial to your success in this interview, so think about it very carefully when you leave here," the Chairman advised and looked around. "Are there any more questions for Mr. Ndoma?"

"Yes, Mr. Ndoma, which part of Simbeck do you come from?" another question was asked.

"I come from south-north," Bondawaa tried to evade the question.

"Mr. Ndoma, please don't be evasive. There are only four regions in this country. You are either from the western area, the north, south or east," the Chairman gave him a lecture.

"I wanted to be precise, I mean my father comes from the south and my mother from the north, I am a child of two regions," Bondawaa defended.

"Good luck Mr. Ndoma, you will hear from us in due course," the Chairman dismissed him. Later, Bondawaa decoded the Chairman's question to mean the number of interviewers bought on his side before him appearing for the interview. He bribed no one before the interview and he was not prepared to do so even after it. The more chances Bondawaa missed of getting a scholarship award, the more depressed he became. He now regarded himself as a big failure and this feeling began to undermine his self-confidence considerably.

One night, Bondawaa found it difficult to sleep. His mind was engaged in analysing this situation and that. That night he questioned the relationship between effort and success in the context of what was operating in Simbeck. In a privileged conversation, a friend told Bondawaa that Simbeck was the world of chimpanzees and monkeys. In that world, the

197

chimpanzees were the laggards, and the monkeys were the hard workers. The monkeys would labour hard for something, and the chimpanzees would come, twist their hands behind their back and take it away from them. The problem with Simbeck was that it was breeding more chimpanzees than monkeys. When a chimp was passing by, all the monkeys around would prostrate, saying, "Yes sir! Good morning, sir! How is the family, sir? Hope everyone is well, sir. Please let me carry your bag for you, sir".

The one-million-dollar question was, "What can be done for the chimps and monkeys to live together without the chimps twisting the monkeys' hands and taking away what they have sweated for?" This question continued to weigh heavily on Bondawaa's mind and the minds of all well-meaning Simbeckians. In his quest to rear a forest of giant trees, Bondawaa had asked himself regularly, "What can I suitably be, a chimp or a monkey?"

That same night, when sleep reluctantly visited Bondawaa, he saw his granddad standing in front of his bed. The old man looked pale and sad. He asked Bondawaa to go with him for a walk. As they were going, the sun was perched at the edge of the horizon before them.

"Do you see that sun? It is going to go down, but it will rise again tomorrow a new sun with different characteristics. With time, those characteristics will repeat themselves. So, it is with the human generation. Help your brethren until your own sun disappears into the horizon. There should always be someone ready

198

to make sacrifices for others, no matter if the sun is shining brightly or not."

"But I hate to fail."

"To fail? A bright sun will eventually go down and darkness will set in, but the marks of that bright sun will not be wiped out from the surface of the earth at once, even by the darkest of night. You will never fail."

"But my friends have all failed me, even some of those I have slaved for endlessly."

"That is the other side of every man's life, disappointment. When the sun starts on its journey, it cannot always be bright from dawn to dusk. Even on the hottest day. When the sun is eclipsed, it will shine bright again." They continued to walk. As they walked along, the sun strode away from them and became redder and redder. "I can see that your heart is getting weaker and weaker, but please beware of the new disease that is weakening the cohesion of our society today - individualism." The old man looked at Bondawaa in the face, squeezed his hand and smiled. He woke up trembling and perspiring profusely.

CHAPTER THIRTY

Keifa Runs for Office

Keifa resigned his post as principal of Ngawobu High to contest for a parliamentary seat in a general election. His sole aim was to become Minister of Education. Before Bondawaa left for the United States, Keifa had told him about his intention to go into national politics.

"I want to find my way into something bigger. I have outgrown this job and the entire environment."

"Don't leave a rat tail for a rat path. Politics is very uncertain. What guarantee do you have of winning the election? Even if you were to win, what are your chances of getting a Ministerial post? Please stay where you are," Bondawaa admonished him.

But our people say, "If you tell a child that there is poo on a palm nut, he will argue that it will not affect the kernel." Keifa could not stop at anything in trying to realize his ambition. National politics was an expensive game. It was even more expensive for people like Keifa who had made their electorates their enemies before going round to ask for their votes.

Looking at the politics of Simbeck critically, the candidate needs to fulfil three conditions to win any general election: to have plenty of money, to have a huge popularity with the youth, and to have connection with the central government. But somebody had advised Keifa that of the three conditions, the

200

candidate needed money most. "You have to pay for every single vote," the person had said.

Keifa took this advice literally, so every single village he and his campaign team went in his constituency; he would ask for the number of voters there and would pay each a thousand Dabras. So, even before the campaign got hot, he was already the most popular candidate of the three in his constituency. When they got to every village, the women would sing his praises:

> *Keifa yo-o our husband yo-o*
> *Keifa yo-o our minister yo-o*
> *Keifa yo-o our saviour yo-o*
> *Keifa yo-o we're all on your side yo-o*
> *Keifa yo-o don't fail us yo-o…*
>
> *Keifa has become a banana leaf*
> *He has surpassed all other leaves*

He would talk about mechanized farming, better education for all, good roads, good housing facilities for the under-privileged and better prices for all local produce. His oratory and witticism were equaled by none of his opponents. He was apparently the victor. Half-educated and inarticulate though he was, the incumbent, Mr. Mundaa Sasei, knew Simbeck politics better than the intellectual Keifa Seppeh-Bengeh, BA, MA, Dip.Ed., former principal of Ngawobu High. He used his money to train thugs, whom he let loose on Keifa and his men on polling day. The thugs ambushed Keifa's men, beat them up and turned all his votes into Sasei's boxes. As if that was not enough, they burnt all houses owned by Keifa; they beat him up and burnt his car too. He lost the election and all his property. And worst of all, he was now out of job. Politics was a bitter, bitter experience for this man, Keifa!

Keifa was not the only victim of election malpractice that year. In the Eastern Province, the Attorney General and Minister of Justice, who was the ruling party's trickster and a man with unlimited power, returned himself and all the party candidates of the constituencies in his district, about six, unopposed. The evening prior to the nomination day, he threw a huge party to which he invited all the dignitaries in the district, including the aspirants of the constituencies there. He said the purpose of the party was to create an informal atmosphere wherein he would talk to all aspirants and their supporters against violence and intimidation in the forthcoming general elections.

As the party progressed, the Attorney General gave an order for the candidates in his district who did not belong to the ruling party, to be rounded up until candidates of his ruling PAPP party had been returned unopposed. From other constituencies there were reports of villages being burnt down, people being killed, cattle massacred, and women raped.

CHAPTER THIRTY-ONE

Bondawaa Goes to United States of America

Bondawaa received a bursary to pursue a Master of Arts degree in folklore at Cornel University, Ithaca, New York, USA. They had put out an advert in a literary journal asking interested persons, preferably Africans, to submit project proposals for this course. "Priority would be given to applicants with the best proposals," the advert said. Apparently, Bondawaa's proposal was ranked among the best, and he was granted the scholarship.

"Oh, how unexpectedly it has turned out!" Bondawaa exclaimed. He shut his eyes in meditation and tears began to run down his cheeks slowly. It was then and only then he realized that over-happiness could be dangerous. It was good that he allowed the tears to run down; otherwise, his heart would have stopped beating. Bondawaa felt good that he was going to the US on his own bat, after a series of disappointments. He felt fulfilled that he was going to the US on sponsorship and was not going to do menial jobs to support himself through college. There in the US he would have the opportunity to grow into a giant tree and rear other giant ones. Yes, he saw his dream standing only a couple of yards away from him.

Before Bondawaa parted company with his mother to board the plane, she whispered to him, "My dear child, whatever sweetness that comes your way in that world, please don't forget about us back at home." For Bondawaa, it was never like going to Gracetown for the first time. He had had much exposure and he was determined to make the best use of this opportunity. But his mother was feeling helpless. She was not sure whether her son would meet her alive after two years, or whether he would be so kind to her by returning immediately after his study programme. Bondawaa was himself not sure, but he was very happy that he was going. He whispered back to his mother, "I know God will keep you alive until I come back. I will be away for only two years. Two years!"

Bondawaa found his stay in the US very rewarding. Though challenging, his master's programme in folklore was enjoyable. It was largely a comparative study. He was looking at folklore in the developed world and folklore in the developing world. There were two striking revelations in his research findings: that folklore tradition in the developing world is sick, almost at the point of death. The more he got immersed in his work, the more he became worried about the state of folklore in the developing world, particularly in Simbeck. In some parts of the developed world huge sums of money were being used to exhume their folklore.

"If we allow ours to die, where shall we get the money from to exhume it?" Bondawaa would ask himself.

In their childhood days, when they returned from the farm in the evening, Bondawaa and his playmates would assemble in the sand in the town square and engage themselves in all kinds of games. These comprised storytelling, riddles, singing, chanting of

nursery rhymes and so on. Their favourite rhyme was
Lolo-o Lolo that went like this:

> *Lolo-o Lolo*
> *Bɔndei piima*
> *Taa Lolo waa ni*
> *Lolo lɔ ngi waa ni*
> *Na nga pɛɛ wa pɛɛ lɔ*
> *Kɛ mugbi a mu kɛ hin*

> *Lolo-o Lolo*
> *The okra plant by the roadside*
> *Was the one that killed Lolo?*
> *It was Lolo who killed the okra plant*
> *Can you do what I can do?*
> *Well, let us all do like this.*

It was a call-to-action rhyme and was always led by
one of the playmates with the others chanting the lines
after him or her. The chorus repeated both the lines
and the actions performed by the lead singer. These
activities were also encouraged in the primary schools,
which led to some amount of continuity between home
and school. But the story is different today, both at
home and in school. Today children are discouraged
from participating in the cultural activities of their
ethnic groups by their parents because they regard
them as primitive and irrelevant to the education and
growth of the children. That is why the folklore in
Simbeck is at the point of death.

One summer day when Bondawaa returned to his
flat, having been thinking of his granddad's warning

the whole day, fearing that "The New Disease" would creep into his heart, especially that he was now living in a country where the extended family system died long ago, his wife gave him a letter from home. The first sentence read:

"Bondawaa, please send me an air ticket to join you in the US, or be ready to fly home for my funeral; politics has left me a battered man."

"Want to read it, Wuyah?" he handed the letter back to his wife.

"Sure, Bondawaa, sure." She read the letter several times, with a sign of confusion on her narrow face.

"Did you not warn your friend about this game before you came?"

"I did, Wuyah, but experience is the best teacher. Now his life has been shattered completely, and he wants an air ticket to join us. What shall we do?"

"What else shall we do? That man is desperate; you had better send him a ticket before he commits suicide. After all, it costs more to fly home to attend a funeral and then fly back, not to talk of other expenses you will incur," Wuyah said.

Bondawaa met Wuyah during his sixth month in the US. It was at a party organized by the Simbeck Students Union there. He fell for her as soon as he saw her. She was in Simbeckian native dress, and her hair was splendidly plaited. She was very beautiful, but from the way she comported herself, Bondawaa knew she was not the type who would make fuss about that

206

quality nature had bestowed upon her. He was sitting close to Wuyah. Each time their eyes met; she would smile in a way that would keep Bondawaa wondering if they had met before.

"I cannot remember the name, but your face resembles one of the many faces I have come across in Kwabu," she said and smiled endearingly.

"I am Bondawaa Ndoma from Ngawobu."

"I am Wuyah Fassiah. My parents live in Kwabu, but they hail from Ngawobu."

Wuyah and Bondawaa enjoyed two months of courtship before they sought the permission of their parents and got married quietly in the church.

When Bondawaa met Keifa at the airport, the latter was a devastated and remorseful man, almost demented. As they embraced Keifa was not able to hold back his tears.

"Bondawaa, thank you very much, I am impressed by your dauntless fraternity," Keifa said in a broken voice.

"Don't mention it, my dear, we should be our brothers' keepers," Bondawaa said, tapping Keifa on the shoulder gently. They walked to the car in eerie silence. As Bondawaa drove, Keifa began to sing a sagacious song:

Miawɔɔ mu na-o
Namia mu na-o

Foh puu bɛɛ
Namia mu na-o

Naa i nɔhɔ bɛɛ
Namia mu na-o

Where we were before
There we are still

Even after ten years
There we shall still be

No matter how filthy it becomes
There we shall still be

Bondawaa's heart began to dance to this astute song, pleased that he was, yet again, playing a role in bringing happiness to a friend that had become a brother.